I0761944

Damsels Distressed: A Collection of Short Stories

By

Rebecka Vigus

ALSO, BY REBECKA VIGUS

MACY MCVANNEL SERIES

Rivers Edge
Crossing the Line
Sanctuary

OTHER NOVELS

Secrets
Out of the Flames
Target of Vengeance
Rescue Mountain

SHORT STORIES

Broken Chains
The Heir
What the Wind Blew In
Escape (A Macy McVannel Story)

CHILDREN'S

Of Moonbeams and Fairies
G is for Gymnastics
Santa is for Real

POETRY

Only a Start and Beyond

NON-FICTION

So, You Think You Want to be a Mommy?

CONTRIBUTING AUTHOR

Tales by the Tree
In Creeps the Night
A Winter's Romance

Damsels Distressed: A Collection of Short Stories

Library of Congress Control Number: 2021909901
Fiction: short stories; mystery, suspense, romance

ISBNs:
Hardcover: 978-1-7372439-1-5
Paperback: 978-1-7372439-0-8
Ebook: 978-1-7372439-2-2

Lilac Publishing
271 Easy St.
Nancy, KY 42544

The Heir originally published July 12, 2015 by Blue Harvest Creative as an Ebook
Broken Chains originally published May 23, 2014 by Blue Harvest Creative as an Ebook
What the Storm Blew In originally published Dec. 14, 2016 by Blue Harvest Creative as an Ebook

To Rick (Rikki) Luke

who gave support so I could continue writing.

You are missed, dear Cousin.

Table of Contents

Stalked

Dedicated to:

Anyone who has ever been stalked.

And It Starts

The phone rings, and everyone in the room jumps. Looking at each other as the phone rings a second time.

Hesitantly I reach for the receiver. "Hello." There is silence on the line. "Hello," I repeat. Still silence. I feel the tension in my body spread to the entire room. Then I hear the "click." Gently I put the phone in its cradle.

There is a brief pause before the phone rings again. This time I am ready. I answer before the second ring. "Hello." Again, the silence. "Good-bye," I say as I hang up the phone.

I am tired of nights like this. Scurrying to get my daughter out the door, before the phone rings again. We pile into the car and she starts asking questions, "Can't they make him stop? Why don't the police do something?"

This is on-going since she stopped seeing Jess six months ago. He started in with the phone calls at all hours. He's about five foot ten inches tall and is a couple years older than she is. But, he is still seeing his old girlfriend and Lacey wants no part of it. Lacey is sixteen and an athlete. She has strawberry-blonde hair and blue eyes. She's an honor student.

I don't have answers for her questions. I only know I need to get away, I don't feel safe. I feel helpless to protect her. Everything feels out of control.

Calmly I answer, "It'll be all right. We're doing everything we can. Right now, we're just getting out of town."

Out of town for us is a two-hour drive to my parents cabin in the woods. We make the drive frequently. Always having a suitcase packed as we will be back in the morning. She has school and I must work.

Six Months Later

Lacey glanced nervously around the parking lot. Her eyes seeking the hauntingly familiar blue car. When she is sure the car is not there, she let out the breath she'd been holding.

Head high Lacey walked into the grocery store mentally chiding herself for her nervousness. This is the first time she'd been home since Jess was sent to jail. He spent a week before his father bailed him out. Then he was put on probation.

It was impossible to think of anyone as funny, unpredictable, and caring as Jess, doing the things he'd done. Terrorizing them for a year before anything was done about it.

She knew he was mad when they broke up. He wanted a serious relationship and she didn't. He didn't understand she felt she was too young for serious. He had two years of college in and was working.

It started with the phone calls. At first, he just hung up. Then there was the silence and the calls came night and day. The phone company wanted a police order. The police told them it wasn't necessary. Her mom was caught in the middle.

Then things got worse. Jess drove by the house at all hours with his stereo blasting so loud the windows shook. He'd park on the shoulder of the road and rev the engine of his car. He started following us everywhere. He followed me to a baby-sitting job and pounded on the door until the neighbors called the police. Jess would park near Mom at the college when she taught nights.

No one seemed to know what he'd do next. Jess was in control and Mom was a nervous wreck. She wasn't sleeping at nights and neither was I. No one wanted to leave the house for fear of what we'd come home to. Mom's biggest nightmare was to drive home and see four-letter words spray painted on the house. Luckily, it never happened. Jess' terrorism was subtler until the night the police caught him at 2 am about to set off fire crackers.

After he did his week in jail, he seemed to disappear. Kacee went to live with an aunt and uncle to work for the summer. Now she was back at school. Things were so much calmer. Mom had the phone number changed.

Author Note

Fear our enemies thrive on it. They find our weaknesses and prey on them. By succumbing to the fear, we fall into a trap. It's what harassers want, they come just short of stalking. They know when you're home and when you're not. They time the harassment for when you're home. It could be hang-up calls, calls with silence on their end or loud music blasting at all hours of the day and night. It could be revving car or motorcycle engines, or squealing tires.

When it starts to escalate, the person starts following you. The problem is, you never know when it's going to happen, so you're always on edge. You snap at loved ones. You cry or rage for seemingly no reason. You pray, for forgiveness for the evil thoughts you have. You even pray for the person stalking you. You hope they will find a better more productive past-time. Finally, you pray it will all end. One day you hope to wake up and it will be over.

The telephone companies are reluctant to tap private phones without a court order. Police can do nothing until they catch the person in the act. Some instances of stalking end up with injury or death to the victim.

If you are being stalked or harassed, tell someone. Tell everyone who will listen. Never go anyplace alone. Be sure people know when you are leaving and where you are going. Let them know when you arrive. Stalking is dangerous for the person being stalked. A PPO-Personal Protection Order- will not stop a stalker. It's just a piece of paper. Police are reluctant to uphold them.

Predator

Dedicated to:

Those who fight evil daily.
May you win more than you lose.

Chapter 1

In the high rise building a woman booted up her laptop, while across town a housewife picked up her child's notebook and began to read. Two women worlds apart yet connected by their children. The woman in the high rise is writing an article for work on parents talking to their teens about Internet predators. The housewife is reading in her teen's notebook about a man she met on-line. Soon the two worlds will collide.

When Your Child Meets Someone in a Chat Room
By Angela Nichols

Parents do you know who your children are chatting with on-line? Do you know what some of their symbols mean? How can you prevent your child from being taken in by a predator?

Last month alone 40,000 children were approached by pedophiles on the Internet. Many of the children have blogs or are on social networks, Tumblr, Facebook, Myspace, Instagram, Twitter, Snapchat, and many more. Do you know what your child is putting on his or her space? Have you seen your child's site?

Some teens are taking sexually provocative photos of themselves. They want to be seen as sexy, special, or exciting. While many are street savvy they are not Internet savvy. Predators are looking at their profiles. Profiles often containing a home address, cell phone number, city they live in, and the school they go to. If your teen is in sports there are sport photos with school colors.

Do you have a set time for your teen to be on-line? Are they in the same room with you or is their computer in their room? Do you have any clue what they are searching on-line? These are important things to know.

Children on-line late at night are big prey. They are lonely or feeling unwanted. They meet someone they believe is the same age and start a conversation. This person understands them completely. Your child might even send this person a photo. The predator will send back a photo, so your child now has a friend. At no time do they realize they are talking with someone older. Someone who is grooming them.

Pedophiles are normal looking people. They hold respectable jobs. Often, they are active in the community. They gravitate to places where there will be children or teens. They offer their time as mentors. They even attend church and have friends. Predators are personable. They blend in and no one suspects.

Then the unthinkable happens, your child disappears. They have arranged to meet their Internet friend. Little do they know they are walking into the arms of a predator. Some of the children will be found before they are harmed. Some will be found after they have been harmed. Then there are those whose bodies turn up later. Finally, there are children who are never found. This is the threat to children unsupervised on the Internet.

Once again, I ask, do you know who your child is chatting with? Do you stalk their pages to see what is on them? If not, take time to talk to them about Internet predators and how they operate. Protect your children.

Angela finished the article, saved it on her flash drive, and placed the flash drive in her bag. She would polish it up in the morning. Now she was going to get a glass of wine and curl up with a book. Then, check on her sleeping children and go to bed. Angela had a son, Trent, who was ten and big into baseball. He had dishwater blond hair, she referred to as bed-head because no matter how often he brushed it, it looked like he just got up. She also had a daughter, Katrina, who was a junior in high school on the fast track for early enrollment in college. Kat was a blonde with brown eyes, she was tall at five feet, seven inches and athletic. She was popular and attended many after school activities. Why just tonight she stayed after to tutor some classmates in chemistry. Angela was proud of who her children were becoming.

She resented the time they spent with their father, but he did make them feel loved. It was the one thing they agreed upon during the divorce, the children would always feel loved by both of them. Steven was supportive. He made sure the child support was paid on time and attended as many of their activities as he could. She stayed in the small apartment because it was in the same school district the kids already were enrolled in. Steven lived elsewhere, but transported them to school daily when he had them. It was a week-on, week-off form of shared parenting. He even took them to doctors' appointments if he had them.

They shared Thanksgiving, but she suspected with Steven's new wife, it would change. Steven took Christmas Eve and brought the children home after mid-night mass, so they could be with Angela for Christmas Day. Other holidays were with whomever the kids were with at the time. It was working.

Across town another mother with tears streaming down her eyes, understood her daughter better than she ever had. She put away the notebook and went to check on her sleeping daughter. When she entered her daughter's room she found the bed made and her daughter missing. There was a note propped against the laptop. She picked it up and read it fearing the worst. Then she made a call to the 9-1-1 operator. The operator spoke to her for five minutes while she waited for the officers to arrive.

Sheila Barton let the officers in. She offered them coffee as she told them about the notebook she found and the note her daughter left when she snuck out of the house. Sheila was terrified her daughter was going to come to harm.

Police asked for a recent photo of her daughter, Amber. When they got one they put out an Amber Alert asking officers check bus stations, air ports, and cab companies. When the Amber Alert went out the news would pick it up right away. They needed to get the photo and description out immediately. There was no telling how long the girl had been gone or how far she had gotten.

Sheila blamed herself for not making more time for her daughter. Since her husband died, she had worked all the extra hours she could to keep them afloat. She never dreamed Amber would get into any trouble.

Amber was a red-head with green eyes and a shining smile. She stood five feet, four inches tall. She had been a cheerleader since ninth grade. She was now a junior. She was academically high in her class, belonging to National Honor Society and doing more volunteer time than she needed to do. According to her friends, she was bubbly and full of life. None had seen or heard from her after 9pm. All seemed surprised she ran off.

Chapter 2

The Amber Alert hit the eleven o'clock news. Amber Barton's picture was splashed on the screen at the beginning to the news. Angela looked up as she put down her wine glass. She'd seen the girl before. Standing she rushed to Kat's room, flipped on the light, and shook her daughter awake.

"Kat, you've got to come with me," she said shaking her daughter's arm.

"Mom?" Kat brushed her hands over her eyes. "What time is it?" she asked.

"Just after eleven, you need to come with me now."

The urgency in her mother's voice finally penetrated her sleepiness. "Okay, Mom, what's going on?"

"Come," Angela said tugging her daughter.

Kat got up grabbed her robe and followed her mom to the living room. Her mom sat down in front of the TV.

"Mom?"

"Just watch the news."

Sitting on the sofa next to her mom, Kat focused her eyes on the TV screen. An Amber Alert flashed right after the ad.

Kat gasped. "Mom, that's Amber Barton!"

"I know, what do you know about her?"

"She was in the tutoring session this afternoon. I heard her talking to someone on the phone after." Kat shook her head, trying to make sense of what she overheard. "She was making plans with someone to meet later. I don't know who."

"We have to call the number they gave. Watch for it." Angela grabbed the newspaper and pen to take the number down.

"There it is 1-800-555-7979," Kat said.

Angela wrote the number, then grabbed her cell phone. She quickly dialed the number.

"This is Angela Nichols, my daughter tutored Amber Barton tonight after school and heard her making plans."

"One moment, while I put you through to the detectives."

"I'm on hold, will you make some coffee?"

Kat nodded and went to the kitchen to start a pot of coffee. She tried to remember everything she heard Amber say. She knew it would be important.

"Yes, yes, please come. 875 East Seventy-Second Street, apartment 4C. I'll buzz you in when you arrive. Thank you." She hung up the phone and turned to Kat. "Do you want to get dressed before they arrive?"

Kat looked down at her pajamas and turned toward her bedroom. When she emerged, she had on jeans and a t-shirt and had brushed her hair pulling it into a ponytail. She reached for the coffee cup her mom held out, knowing Mom made her hot chocolate. They sat on the sofa to wait for the police to arrive.

Less than ten minutes the police showed up. Angela buzzed them in and opened the door to them after they identified themselves.

"Would either of you like coffee or hot chocolate?" she asked leading them into the kitchen where Kat had moved.

"Coffee for me, Ma'am," responded the male officer.

"Hot chocolate if you have it ready," responded the female.

"Sit right down, I have both." She grabbed two mugs filled on with coffee and the other hot chocolate. "Kat, do you need a refill?"

"Yes, please," she answered.

Angela brought the two mugs to the table and filled Kat's hot chocolate from a pan. She filled her own mug with coffee and said, "Cream and sugar are both on the table." Then she sat next to her daughter.

"I'm Officer John Bradley and this is my partner, Officer Jessie Marsh. We're here to follow up on a call you made to a tip line about our Amber Alert."

"I made the call," Angela told them.

Officer Bradley looked her in the eye, "Do you something about her disappearance?"

"No, but my daughter might."

He turned to look at Kat. "And you are?"

"I'm Katrina Nichols. I tutored Amber after school today." Kat told them.

"What can you tell us?" he prompted.

"She seemed distracted during our session and I heard her on the phone as she was leaving," Kat replied. "She said she was going to try and get away. Then asked where she should meet him. Before I could say anything, she was gone."

"Do you tutor her often?" Officer Bradley asked.

"I tutor twice a week after school for National Honor Society. The kids who need help in chemistry come to me. Amber has come regularly for the past two weeks. I'm not sure why she's coming, because sometimes she can explain it better than I can."

"Is she close to anyone in the group? Is there a young man there she might be seeing?"

Kat thought for a minute. "I don't think so. She's a cheerleader but, doesn't hang out with jocks. Most of the guys in my group are athletes trying to keep themselves eligible to play sports. I don't see her with any of them during school."

"Is there anything else you can tell us?" he pressed.

"Not really. I see her in the halls, but she is always alone. I rarely see her on her cell phone. It's what struck me as odd today. She's more of a loaner and not into selfies," Kat told them. "I wish I knew her better."

Officer Marsh spoke for the first time, "This is my card. If you think of anything or hear anything, please call me at any time." She handed a card to Kat and one to Angela.

The officers stood. Officer Bradley spoke to Angela, "Thank you for calling and for the coffee." He turned to Kat saying, "Believe it or not, you've been a big help. Do you by any chance have Amber's cell number?"

"I do, let me get my phone." Kat dashed to her bedroom and came back carrying her phone. "Her number is 202-555-5599."

"Thank you," replied Officer Marsh as she wrote the number in a small notebook. Then they left.

Angela hugged Kat. "Go back to bed, Sweetie."

"Not sure I can sleep, but I'll rest," Kat replied heading to her room still carrying a mug of hot chocolate.

Turning to the table, Angela gathered up the mugs and took them to the sink to wash. All the time thinking, *this could have been one of my children. It's like the article I wrote tonight. Maybe tomorrow I'll see if I can do an interview with Mrs.*

Barton. Hopefully by then Amber will be back and this will just be a mini nightmare.

Turning out the light she checked on Trent, noted Kat still had her light on and went to bed.

Chapter 3

Kat found herself thinking about Amber. She should have known something was up. The girl rarely ever had her cell phone out. She was cute but, didn't seem to know it and she was smart. Kat never understood why she came for tutoring sessions. She could have been a tutor.

Wondering which of her friends might have a class with Amber, she scrolled through her phone list. None of her friends ever mentioned her. Weird, had she always been in school with them?

Getting out of bed, Kat pulled her junior high and high school yearbooks. She paged through them looking for Amber in any of the photos. When she didn't find them, she paged to the back where it listed those who had been missing on picture day.

Amber did not show up until ninth grade. It made Kat wonder where she had been before. Usually new kids were spotted right off. But Amber didn't stick out. You could go for weeks and not even notice her. Except she was on the cheer team. Odd, no one included her in the cheer team gatherings. Or at least she didn't attend them.

Puzzled, Kat climbed back into bed, pulled up the covers, and turned out the light. She still had school in the morning, however she found herself tossing and turning. Her dreams were of Amber and made no sense. She slept fitfully until her alarm went off.

Sheila Barton paced her apartment. The officer who stayed with her, told her other officers went to talk to a classmate who had called the tip line. She didn't recognize the name of the girl. Sadly, she knew very few of Amber's friends. Come to think of it, she wasn't even sure Amber had any friends.

She prayed the girl could give them an idea of who Amber had gone to meet and where. She tried to do everything right. This apartment had been cheaper than the one they lived in before her husband died. It's why she moved here and why she worked two jobs.

She let out a big sigh and settled on the worn sofa. Pulling an afghan around her as if it could give warmth and strength. When Amber got back, Sheila would do everything possible to make her a priority and not the work.

In the meantime, she needed to know who this person was, her daughter ran off to meet. *Was he really someone her age or was he a predator?* Sheila was terrified. She prayed the phone would ring. She wanted to wake in the morning to this being just a bad dream.

She headed toward the kitchen to make coffee. As she passed the officer she asked, "Would you like something, coffee, water, tea?"

"Tea, if it's not too much trouble," the woman replied. "Then maybe we can look at your daughter's diary again."

Sheila nodded. They had taken her daughter's laptop, hopefully there would be a clue there. It was past midnight.

Amber had never stayed out this late before. She busied herself making coffee and tea. It was going to be a very long night.

The ringing of the phone made Sheila jump. She looked at the officer. The officer nodded, and Sheila made her way to pick up the phone.

"Hello," she said nervously.

"Mrs. Barton, this Cyndy Colepepper with TV8 news. Do you have time do an interview?"

The officer took the phone, "Get off this line. We are keeping it open for Amber Barton." She hung up. "I'm sorry, Mrs. Barton."

Sheila returned to the task of getting them drinks then sat next to the officer. "I'm sorry. With everything going on, I didn't catch your name."

"Officer Madilynn James, you can call me Madi," she replied.

"Thank you, Madi, but only if you will call me Sheila."

"Agreed."

As Madi sipped her tea, Sheila asked, "Do you get called to do this often?"

"More often than I like," she answered. "Usually it's runaways and mostly they call to come home. I think this is different. Amber has a connection to the person she refers to in her diary."

"Unfortunately, I don't know who it is," Sheila explained. "I've been working two jobs since my husband died. We downsized where we live, and Amber had to change schools. I thought she had adjusted."

"You can't beat yourself up," Madi assured her. "Kids her age are good at hiding how they feel."

Sheila shrugged, "Still I should have paid more attention. I should have been the one she turned to, not some stranger." She began to cry again.

Madi feeling helpless could only pat Sheila's hand. She couldn't promise it would be okay. Not until they had Amber home, if she came home.

Chapter 4

Kat was up early to see the news. She wanted to hear Amber Barton had been found and was back home. Her phone lit up with text messages as soon as she turned it on. She answered one after another as she got ready for the day.

Trix: Did u hear about Amber?

Kat: Yes, any news?

Trix: just rumor

Kat: K

Mickey: Update on Amber?

Kat: No

Mickey: She ran off with some guy?

Kat: No idea

Max: she in ur class?

Kat: yea

Max: know her?

Kat: not well

Max: weird

Kat: yea

Max: Hey Amber Alert on Amber...Ha ha!

Turning off her phone she headed to the kitchen to find her mom already there and making breakfast.

"I didn't know how early you would be up," Angela said. "So, I started breakfast. Pancakes okay?"

"Sure, I guess."

"I heard your phone going off," Angela told her. "Any good news?"

"No, just rumors."

Angela put a plate of pancakes in front of Kat, who put butter on each one and poured maple syrup over them. She ate almost mechanically, almost as if in a trance.

Looking up at her mom, she knew something bad was going to happen. Somehow, she felt as though she should have been able to stop it. If only she had paid more attention. “Mom, is this my fault?”

“Why would you think it was your fault?”

“I didn’t make any effort to get to know her. I just tutored her,” Kat replied. “Then I didn’t try to catch up to her when I heard her on the phone. Maybe I could have done something to stop her from going.” Tears rolled down Kat’s face.

Angela went to her daughter and hugged her. “Baby, you couldn’t have stopped this. If it was an Internet predator, he has been grooming her for months to run away. If it’s just a boyfriend, they will come back soon. Either way, it’s not your fault.”

Kat shrugged and finished her breakfast. After putting her dishes in the dishwasher, she picked up her bookbag and headed out the door to school. She knew it was going to be a long day. Even though her mom said it wasn’t her fault, Kat believed she should have done more. Who knows, maybe she would still get the chance.

When the phone rang both Sheila and Officer Jones jumped. As Sheila picked it up, Madilynn turned on the recorder and set a trace.

Sheila hesitated then said, “Hello.”

"Mom, I hate it here I want to come home," Amber whispered.

"Just tell me where you are, and I'll come," Sheila replied.

"I don't know," Amber sniffed as she answered. "It's not like I thought it would be. I'm sending you his photo. Please hurry."

"Okay, baby, just don't turn off your phone. I love you."

"I love you, too, Mom." The line went dead.

"You were great, Sheila. We have a fix on her I'm going to call it in, so we can get people there," Officer Jones told her.

"Wait, Amber sent me his photo," Sheila said checking her inbox. "Here it is." She held her phone to Madilynn.

Taking the phone, Madilynn quickly sent the text to her boss with an explanation this was the kidnapper. Now all they could do was wait.

"I pray she left the phone on," Sheila said.

"Me, too," Madilynn returned to the computer screen. "It hasn't moved from this location. Which is a really good sign."

Too pent up to just sit, Sheila headed for the kitchen. "Madilynn, do you like scrambled eggs. I usually put bacon and cheese in them."

"Sounds great!"

Sheila began making the bacon. When it was done, and lying on a paper towel, she started the eggs, adding the bacon, and stirring. As the eggs were getting close to done, she added shredded cheddar and mozzarella cheeses to the mix. She turned down the heat and put bread in the toaster. She buttered the toast when it came up and put the eggs onto two plates. Then she carried them to the table.

"Is there anything else I can get you?"

"How about another cup of tea?'

As Sheila turned to start the tea, the phone rang again. She turned almost in slow motion to answer it. Again, as she picked up the phone Madilynn put a tracer on it and started recording.

"Hello."

"Mom," she said in a whisper.

"Amber?"

"He hurt me. I think he's gone, but I'm not sure I'm going to make it."

"Amber, help is coming. Amber, Amber!"

Madilynn said, "The line is open, but she's not answering." She picked up her phone and dialed her commander. "Sir, we have the girl on the line. She's been injured and tells us the man is gone. What is your ETA?"

"We are outside the house now. I have men breaching the door and an ambulance is just down the street."

"Roger, that," Madilynn said. She looked at Sheila, "They're there, Ma'am."

Sheila nodded holding the phone like a life line.

"Get the ambulance attendants in here pronto! This is bad," said a male voice over the phone.

Madilynn grabbed the phone from Sheila and hung it up. "They are with her, Sheila. She's safe now."

Numbly Sheila nodded.

“Sit here I’m going to get you some tea.” She guided Sheila to a chair. “Do you have any whiskey?”

“The cupboard on the left,” Sheila responded.

Looking Madilynn found the whiskey, she turned on the burner and made sure there was water in the tea pot. She found the tea bags and put one in a cup. When she could hear the water boiling, she poured it over the tea bag and turned off the burner. She added a generous dash of whiskey, some cream she found in the fridge and carried it to Sheila. “Drink up and I’ll find out where they are taking her for medical treatment.”

Sheila looked at the cup, then brought it to her mouth to drink. It went down smoothly warming her from the inside out. Her daughter had been found. She was going to get medical help. They would get through this.

Chapter 5

Kat sat through the entire day of school hoping to hear something besides rumors about Amber. She was disappointed by the way her friends were passing judgement on a girl they barely knew.

Then, the first breaking news came across her phone. It was a photo of a man suspected in Amber's disappearance. She enlarged the photo. This was a man she'd seen before. Now, if she could only remember where.

While she was thinking about the man a second breaking news came across her feed. Amber had been found but, was raced to a hospital. No further news was known.

The phone started blowing up with texts.

Trix: Have we seen that guy?

Kat: Think so. Where?

Max: Do you know what hospital?

Kat: No

Mickey: Guy is creepy.

Kat: yeah

Trix: Malt shop on 59th?

Kat: That's it!!

She moved to dial and called the number the officer had given her last night.

"Officer Marsh."

"This is Kat Nichols, I've seen the man in the photo."

"Where, Kat?"

"Malt shop on 59th. He was always watching us."

"Good, stay away from there for a couple of days, so we can get him."

"Right." Kat disconnected. She was heading home.

Max: Is that the guy from the Malt shop?

Kat: Yeah, stay away.

Max: Why?

Kat: Let cops handle it.

Max: No way

Kat: Max, promise

There was no response from Max. Kat continued home. She was more concerned about Amber than Max doing something stupid. Maybe she and Mom could keep Mrs. Barton company at the hospital. She texted her mom: On way home. Can you find out what hospital Amber is in? We could go there.

Mom: Checking. See you at home.

She made her way home and did homework while waiting for her mom. Kat felt edgy. When her brother got home she made him a grilled cheese sandwich and helped him with his homework. He really didn't need the help, but Kat was too nervous to be alone.

Mom walked in and found them with their heads together over Trent's homework. "Does he really need help?"

"No, Mom," Kat replied looking up. "I just needed to do something."

Her mom gave her a hug and sent her son off to his games. Then, she turned to Kat saying, "She's in Our Savior Hospital. We can go after dinner."

"Can we stop and get her flowers or something?"

“Sure, we can. Now, set the table for dinner and we’ll be able to get there sooner.”

Kat went about setting the table while her mom heated leftovers and made a tossed salad. She went to find Trent for dinner. He was engrossed in a video game but, came as soon as she told him it was ready.

After dinner, Kat cleared the table and her mom made arrangements for Trent to spend a couple hours with his dad. Then, Kat and Angela left for the hospital. On the way, they stopped to pick up flowers, a card, a coffee for Amber’s mom, and a teddy bear. They asked at the information desk where they could find Amber Barton.

“I’m sorry she’s still in surgery. You can wait in the lounge on the surgical floor if you’d like. I’ll have one of our volunteers show you how to get there.” She motioned for a young girl. “Will you take these ladies to the surgical lounge, please?”

“Sure, follow me.” The girl turned and led the way to a bank of elevators. “Take this to the fourth floor and turn right when you get there. The lounge will be right through the double doors.”

Angela nodded and said, “Thanks.” Then pushed the up button for the elevator.

It didn’t take long to get the elevator. They entered and pushed the button for the fourth floor. Neither spoke on the quick ride up. They stepped off the elevator and turned right. They walked through the doors to see a woman and a police officer sitting there. The officer looked up.

“May I help you, ladies?”

"We came to sit with Mrs. Barton," Angela replied. Holding out the cup she said, "We stopped to get her something besides hospital coffee."

The officer motioned them over. She turned to Mrs. Barton and said, "Sheila, these ladies want to keep you company. Is that okay?"

Slowly Sheila Barton looked up. She smiled wanly as Angela handed her the coffee, "Thank you, please sit. I'm Sheila Barton."

"I'm Angela Nichols and this is my Katrina. She and Amber are classmates."

"You know my daughter?" Sheila asked looking at Kat.

"She came to my science tutoring class, I was hoping to get her to tutor with me."

"Amber has always excelled in science. Please join me. There has been no word."

Angela and Kat pulled chairs closer to Sheila. Kat put the flowers and teddy bear on an empty chair. They made small talk and prayed while they waited.

After what seemed like forever a doctor came out to talk to Mrs. Barton. Kat and her mom stood but did not approach the doctor, only Mrs. Barton did.

"She has come through surgery however, the next twenty-four hours will tell us if she's going to make it," the doctor said.

"You might as well go home and get some rest. We'll call you if there is a change."

"I'm not leaving this hospital," Sheila told him. "You have my baby in there. I'll stay until she is out of the woods."

"As you wish, there is a more comfortable lounge on the third floor outside the Intensive Care Unit." He nodded to the others and left.

"Of all the rude…" Kat started.

Angela stopped her with a nod. "We'll stay with you, Sheila."

Sheila nodded, and they left for the elevators and the third floor. Kat remembered to bring the flowers and teddy bear.

On the third floor, they were stopped at the nurses' station. "We can put those in water for you, but they are not allowed in ICU," the nurse told them. Our waiting room is this way." She stepped from behind the desk to show them. "We have coffee and tea. Our kitchen staff will bring breakfast sandwiches, sandwiches for lunch, but no dinner. Two of the sofas pull out. I'll find some bedding for you. What patient are you here for?"

Officer James spoke, "Amber Barton. This is her mother, Sheila." She pointed to Sheila. "These are friends who have come to comfort her, Mrs. Nichols and her daughter, Kat."

"Visiting hours won't start until 9am. I'll see if I can find you some food for tonight if you'd like," the nurse offered.

Angela spoke up, "I'll make a run out for food as soon as we get settled. Thank you."

The nurse nodded and left. She returned a few minutes later carrying sheets, blankets, and pillows. Angela and Kat made up one sofa bed and told Sheila to use it. Then, they made up the other sofa bed for themselves. Finally, they made a make shift bed on a sofa which didn't pull out for Officer James.

Officer James had stepped into the hall to make a phone call. "Captain," she said. "Amber Barton is out of surgery. She has survived, but from what the doctor said it can go either way in the next twenty-four hours. A friend of Amber's from school and her mother are here, is there anyway someone can stop and get take-out for us? I'm staying because a reporter called the house earlier and I don't want them bothering Mrs. Barton."

"Any particular kind of take-out? Good thinking about staying. I'll get you relief in the morning and you can take the day off."

"I'll ask about the food." She walked back to the waiting room. "Ladies, we are going to have take-out delivered. What would you like?"

Sheila said, "Can it be Chinese?"

"Sure can. Anyone else?"

Kat replied, "I'd like moo goo gai pan."

Angela said, "Chicken and broccoli, please."

Madi looked at Sheila, "Crab rangoons with hot mustard and red sauce like for egg rolls, and moo shoo chicken."

She gave the orders to her chief adding crab rangoons for all and chicken fried rice. Hanging up the phone she said, "We should have delivery in half an hour. They'll bring us Chinese tea, fortune cookies, and Cokes."

They settled into their respective sofas to wait. Once everyone had eaten, they turned off most of the lights in the waiting room and tried to sleep.

Kat thought she heard people coming in during the night. Once she thought someone tucked a blanket around her. But, she slept until she heard the breakfast cart rattle in.

Kat stretched trying not to wake her mom. She slowly sat up. Officer James was gone. Her sofa had blankets and a pillow on it. Her mom and Mrs. Barton seemed to be sleeping. She eased her way out of bed and over to find breakfast. She was surprised to see scrambled eggs, bacon, and sausage. There were fruit cups, orange and apple juice, and the ever-present coffee. Kat helped herself and went to sit at the only table in the waiting room. Soon her mom began to stir and so did Mrs. Barton. Kat suspected a nurse would be in soon to take Mrs. Barton to see Amber.

That's when the alarm went off. The speaker system announced Code Blue. Nurses and doctors came scrambling from everywhere. Her mom was on her feet in an instant. It took Mrs. Barton a minute to orient herself, then she was rushing to the door. She opened it to find a police officer standing there.

"Wait here, Ma'am. I'll see if you can see your daughter," the officer told her.

"Mom, what's going on?" Kat asked forgetting her breakfast.

"I think someone is in trouble," Angela replied. She stepped over to hug her daughter.

The hall got quiet. The officer returned to the doorway, "Mrs. Barton, it will be a few minutes. They are working on a patient and no one is allowed in yet. Why don't you get some breakfast?"

Without responding Sheila turned back into the waiting room. First, she made her bed and put the sofa back together. Then, she got some breakfast and joined Kat.

Angela made up the other sofa and put it back into a sofa instead of a bed. She got coffee and something to eat joining her daughter and Sheila. Nothing was said as they ate.

Down the hall doctors were working frantically to save Amber Barton. She started with convulsions, then they discovered bleeding. It looked like she would be back in surgery if they could get her stabilized. Things were not looking good for Amber's future.

Finally, she seemed to be breathing on her own. They decided to let her mom in for a few minutes before they took her to surgery. There was no guarantee she would make it through another surgery.

A nurse came into the waiting room. She looked around trying to figure out which of the two women was Mrs. Barton. Finally, she asked, "Mrs. Barton, will you come with me?"

Sheila stepped forward to follow the nurse. Kat picked up her dishes and threw them away, then walked to her mom, "This isn't good, is it?"

"I don't think so," her mom acknowledged.

Kat busied herself picking up the breakfast trays. She got her mom a fresh cup of coffee. Finally, she sat.

Sheila came back ten minutes later. Tears streamed down her cheeks. Angela went to her saying, "What is it, Sheila?"

Sheila sat on the nearest sofa. "They are taking her back to surgery. They don't know if she will survive another one so soon. They told me to say good-bye, but I couldn't. I told her I'd be waiting for her when she woke up."

"Good for you," Angela said. "You don't give up on her. She's a fighter. She called for help."

Sheila just nodded. Angela hugged her. Kat watched in silence.

Time seemed to crawl. At some point sandwiches were brought in for lunch. More coffee was provided along with bottled water and pop. No one had much appetite, but they forced themselves to eat.

Angela said, "No news is good news." Although she was no longer sure she believed it.

Someone had turned on the television to an all-news channel. The volume was turned down as no one seemed interested on anything outside this room.

A chaplain from the hospital came in to sit with them and offer comfort. He went through the effort of praying with them, but no one really seemed to hear his words. He left as silently as he arrived.

Kat found some cards and started playing solitaire. It was something to do so she didn't think about Amber. Yet, her mind roamed to Amber. She thought of all the opportunities she had to reach out to the girl and didn't. Somehow, she had to make this right. Silently she prayed Amber would be okay and they could somehow become friends. She looked at the little bear she picked out. It should have been more than a bear. It should have said something about caring. But, there it was, a little teddy bear. She threw the cards and began to pace.

Chapter 6

Word came two hours later, Amber had survived surgery. They were waiting for the next twenty-four hours to pass before they would make any further prognosis.

Angela said, “I need to get home and check on Trent. I also need to do a follow up on an article I wrote last week. Kat, do you want to come with me or do you want to stay with Sheila?”

“I’m going to stay with Mrs. Barton if it’s alright,” Kat replied.

“Okay, Sheila, do you want me to stop by your apartment and pick up some fresh clothes for you?”

Sheila dug in her purse, “Here’s the key. I don’t care what you pick to bring me. Thanks.” She pressed the key into Angela’s hand and held it there for a moment.

Angela left. The officer on duty was not friendly like Officer James had been. Just stood outside the waiting room, keeping out those who were with the press.

The day dragged on, lunch came and went. Still Kat stayed with Mrs. Barton. Maybe out of guilt, maybe because she had nowhere else to go. She turned off her phone, so she wouldn’t have to hear the stupid comments from her friends. It made her think about the people she called friends. She picked up her phone to see if her mom had called. There were too many messages to even begin to answer. No call or text from her mom, so she turned it off again.

“It’s okay if you want to call or text your friends,” Sheila told her.

"No, I don't want to text them," Kat answered. "They are being stupid about this whole thing."

"Probably, it's the only way they know how to handle it."

Kat shrugged. "I think they need to step back and put themselves in this position."

"Don't be too hard on them. They are your friends."

Lunch was wheeled in. Sheila and Kat walked over to check it out. Then the nurse came in.

"Mrs. Barton?" she asked.

"Me," Sheila answered turning from the food tray.

"If you'd come with me, please," she turned toward the door.

Kat squeezed Sheila's hand as she followed the nurse out the door. The next thing Kat heard was a piercing scream as if someone had been stabbed. She dropped the paper plate she was holding and ran to the door. She was just in time to see the nurse help Sheila to a chair. A doctor was standing there. Kat didn't think twice, she ran to Sheila's side.

Angela came off the elevator and heard the scream. She went running toward the waiting room and saw Kat running to Sheila. She just kept on going. A nurse stepped to stop her.

"Please, talk to your sister. There is nothing else we can do for your niece," she said urgently. "Get her to sign the organ donor release form." She let go of Angela and walked away.

Angela moved on to where Kat and Sheila were. Sheila was sobbing and unable to speak. Kat held her shoulder, so she wouldn't fall off the chair they found for her. Tears ran down her face as she realized the gravity of the situation.

"Can we have a moment, please?" Angela asked the waiting hospital personnel. "Amber is her only child."

Nurses, orderlies, and doctors backed away. Angela took Sheila by the arm and helped her stand. Between the two of them Kat and Angela got Sheila back to the waiting room.

"Kat, find some coffee and a bottle of water."

"Sure, Mom," Kat was glad to have something to do.

Angela took off her coat and sat next to Sheila. "What exactly did they tell you?"

Sheila was crying and took a minute to get herself under control. After a deep sigh she said, "Amber has gone into a coma and there is no brain activity. They want me to sign some papers, I'm not even sure what for."

She took the papers from Sheila and said, "I'll look at them."

Kat arrived with the coffee and the water. Angela took the coffee and out of her bag produced a bottle of whiskey. She poured a liberal amount in and handed the cup to Sheila. "Drink this, it will help."

Sheila drank. Kat was astounded to find her mother carrying booze in her bag. She wondered if this was a regular occurrence.

When Sheila finished the coffee, she handed the cup to Kat who took it to the waste basket. Angela handed Sheila the bottle of water and began looking at the papers.

"Sheila, I want us to go and see Amber," Angela said. "Then, we will talk about these papers and what they mean."

They left the waiting room and headed to the nurses' station. When they arrived a nurse asked, "May I help you?"

Angela answered, "We'd like to see Amber now."

"Right this way." The nurse led them to Amber's bedside.

She was hooked up to more tubes and IV's than Angela thought anyone could be attached to. Sheila took her daughter's hand. Tears ran slowly down her face. It was the first time she'd seen Amber since she went missing.

"Who could do this to a child?" she whispered.

"Only a monster," Angela replied. "I'm going to step out, so you can be alone with her and tell her how much you care."

"Please, don't go," Sheila said. She pulled a chair up next to her daughter. "Amber, I so wish you had talked to me before going off with this man. I wish we could have more time together. I love you more than life itself. But, I know Dad is waiting for you."

She looked at Angela, "I'll sign the papers now. I understand what they were trying to say. Will you and Kat stay with me to the end?"

"Of course, we will. Let me go get the papers."

Angela left to get the papers and Kat. Together they returned to Amber's room. Sheila took the papers and signed them. Angela took them to the nurses' station.

The nurse took them and said, "I'll have the doctor paged. You can stay as long as you'd like."

"Thank you," Angela replied, then turned to head back to the room.

There was silence in the room Sheila held Amber's hand on one side and Kat held her other one. Angela went to stand by Kat. She put her arms around her daughter. "I'm so sorry."

It was not long before the doctor and the nurse entered the room. The nurse asked, "Would you like to have a chaplain with you?"

"Is there one available?" Sheila asked.

"Yes, we have one here in the hospital. I'll make the call." She left the room as the doctor removed IV's.

The nurse returned with a chaplain and began removing the leads to the heart monitor, as well as other tubes, connected to Amber.

Then the doctor said, "Mrs. Barton, if you are ready I will turn of the breathing machine."

Sheila nodded. Then, said, "Go ahead."

The machine was turned off. Amber did not struggle for breath. The chaplain said a prayer which none of them heard. The words seemed soothing and then it was over. Amber's chest did not rise and fall anymore. The nurse, doctor, and chaplain left the room quietly.

Kat turned to her mom and cried. Sheila looked at them both as she let go of her daughter's hand.

"Thank you, both for being here."

"It's the least we could do. Will you need help with arrangements? Angela asked.

Sheila looked numb, "I would be forever grateful to you, if you have the time."

"We will make the time."

Together the three of them left the hospital room. They stopped at the nurses' station to ask when the body would be released. The answer was by the end of the day.

They made a stop in the waiting room to gather their belongings and then left the hospital together. Kat drove while her mother contacted a funeral home giving them directions to pick up Amber's body from the hospital. She gave them her number as a call back and said they would arrive in a couple of hours to pick out a casket and make arrangements.

Sheila sat in the back with tears running down her face. Her loss too great for words.

Chapter 7

Calls were made, and family began showing up about three in the afternoon, by five it was on the early news and neighbors arrived with food, by six the news cameras were in front of the house, and by seven a candle light vigil had begun in the front lawn. Flowers, balloons, stuffed toys, signs, and candles appeared. Someone brought a cross and people placed things around it.

Kat didn't get it. Not one of these kids had reached out to the "new kid." Yet, here they were all mourning her death. She'd shut off her phone after the early news. The texts from her friends were pathetic.

Max: Hey, did u see her?

Kat: Yes

Max: Was it gross?

Kat: Seriously?

Trix: Did she leave a note?

Kat: It wasn't suicide.

Mickey: Heard they were cutting her up.

Kat: Organ donation, it's a good thing.

Trix: Candle vigil tonight at 7. U b there?

Kat: Where is there?

Trix: Her mom's

Kat: Already here.

Then she just stopped answering. *What was Max thinking, was it gross?* Kat shook her head and went to the kitchen to see if she could help her mom. They had been playing hostesses ever since Sheila's family started showing up.

Her mom and Sheila were in the den making the final arrangements for Amber's funeral when the first of the family arrived. Sheila had been in a fog ever since. Sometimes she would hold Kat's hand as if it anchored her to the world. Other times she sobbed uncontrollably.

The kitchen had slowed down a bit when they heard someone from the living room say, "Come look at this."

Kat and Angela made their way to the living room where people were crowded around the front window and door. The candle light vigil had started. About an hour later, guests began to leave. Kat and her mom cleaned up the kitchen and Angela helped Sheila to her room. They locked the door on their way out. Angela had called ahead for a taxi and it was waiting. It was a silent ride home.

Once there, Kat went straight to her bedroom. She changed her clothes, plugged in her phone, put it on vibrate, and went to bed. She was asleep by the time her head hit the pillow.

Kat awoke to the smell of bacon. Her mom was cooking, something she rarely did anymore. She roused herself, went to the bathroom, took a shower, dressed, and went to the kitchen.

"Just in time," Angela told her. "I made your favorites, scrambled eggs, bacon, and toast. I even have orange juice to go with your coffee."

Smiling Kat brought a steaming cup of coffee to her nose, so she could inhale the aroma, then she put it down and added milk and sugar. Finally, it was ready to drink. She took a big drink before sitting down at the table.

"So, did you sleep well?"

"I think so, I don't remember dreaming."

"Your friend, Trix, called me this morning because you weren't answering your phone or texts," her mom said.

"What did you tell her?"

Angela replied, "You were still sleeping, and I'd have you call or text her later."

"I don't even want to look at my texts."

"Why not?"

"Mom, really?" Kat sighed. "None of them knew her. They didn't try to be her friend. It's all just fake grief." She shuddered. "It makes me sick."

"The horrific loss of a classmate, whether they knew her or not, is causing them to think twice about their lives," her mom explained. "They wonder if they have done something which might come back on them at some point. Besides, the police are still looking for the man she went off with."

Shrugging her shoulders, as she chewed her breakfast, Kat was quiet. Then she said, "I guess this will be news for a while. It's really sad. She didn't have to die. It was so senseless."

"I agree." Angela sat down next to Kat at the kitchen counter. "This is going to be even harder, my article on Internet predators comes out today. I've been asked to do a follow-up in light of Amber's death."

"You have to do what your bosses tell you," Kat replied. "I can understand. I just hope you can put a human side to your story."

"After spending time with Sheila, I'm sure I can. In fact, I'm going to ask her to help me with the story," she said.

"Awesome, idea, Mom!"

"Thanks, I have some good ones once in a while." She hugged Kat and went to change into her work clothes. "You stay here and rest today. The funeral tomorrow is going to take its toll."

"I will. I'm just going to lounge around here," Kat replied. "I'll even text Trix."

Chapter 8

After her mother left, Kat checked her text messages. Finally, she decided to text Trix.

Kat: Sup?

Trix: Where u been?

Kat: Sleeping

Trix: News is school will close for funeral

Kat: Why?

Trix: So, classmates can attend

Kat: Skip day

Trix: pretty big turnout I think

Kat: Whateva

Trix: Y u so weird about this?

Kat: Not weird not fake

Trix: fake?

Kat: E1 pretending to be her friend

Trix: u mean the vigil?

Kat: yah that, too

Trix: didn't see u there

Kat: I was inside the house

Trix: y

Kat: helping out

Trix: Did u know her?

Kat: yah, a little

Trix: Oh

Kat: gotta go door

She put her phone back on vibrate and turned on the TV. At least she might be able to find some mindless show to watch so she didn't think about Amber. As she was scrolling through the channels, she heard a knock at the door.

"Who is it?" Kat asked.

"Officer Madi James."

"Wait just a minute." Kat began unlocking the door.

Officer James and another officer were waiting. Kat stepped back allowing them into the apartment.

"What can I do for you?" she asked.

"Kat, we need to talk," Madi began. "I called your mom at the paper and she said you were home."

"Sure, what do you need?" asked Kat.

Madi handed her a manila folder, "Anything you can tell me about that man."

"Let's sit down," Kat said as she walked into the living room. She took the picture out of the folder. "This is the guy who was on TV."

"Yes, Amber sent us his photo."

"Wow!"

"What?" Madi asked.

"He used to hang around the coffee shop we went to after school. I thought it was weird, he was the only guy over twenty who was ever there."

"Was he there often?"

"Like every day," Kat said. "He would stare at us. I thought he was creepy. We joked about him and never left anyone sitting alone or walking alone."

"Not even Amber?" Madi pressed Kat to think.

"Nope." Kat thought for a moment then said, "I remember walking with Amber one day. We talked about how creepy the guy was. She thanked me for not leaving her alone. Funny, I forgot it until you asked."

"It's okay," Madi said. "You've been through quite a lot. We'd prefer it if you still didn't go anyplace alone. We want this guy in custody."

Kat said nothing. Madi could tell she was thinking about something. When she finally spoke, she shocked both officers.

"You look young enough. If we put you in street clothes, you could come to the coffee shop with me. Maybe we could catch him there," Kat said.

Madi was too startled to respond. Her partner said, "She might be onto something, Madi."

Nodding Madi, let the idea sink in. "I have to talk to my boss. Tell me you are staying in today, Kat."

"I am. I don't want to deal with my classmates today. Tomorrow at the funeral will be soon enough," Kat answered. "Hey, do you think he might show up at the funeral? With the crowd of kids turning out, he could just mix with the crowd."

"We'll look into having plainclothes officers at the funeral," Madi assured her. "For now, I'm going to talk to my boss about your idea. I need your phone number, so I can call you when I have an answer."

Kat quickly gave Madi her cell phone number. She walked the two officers to the door and locked it when the left. She shuddered, nope not going anywhere alone. She wondered how often the man had followed Amber home. How did he get in touch with her and why did she go with him? Too, many questions. Kat went to the kitchen to make some lunch.

She dozed off after lunch and was startled awake by the ringing from her cell phone.

"Hello," she answered sleepily.

"Kat, it's Officer James. My boss says we can try me going with you to the coffee shop the day after the funeral. I'll pick you up after school."

"Meet me at school, but we need to walk to the coffee shop. We don't want him to see us pull up in a cop car, not even an unmarked one."

"Okay, I'll text you at the end of the day to let you know where I am."

"Sounds good."

For the first time since Amber disappeared, Kat felt like she was doing something for Amber. It felt good, in a sad kind of way. She kept beating herself up for all the missed opportunities to know Amber better. Maybe she could have stopped her from running away. Would she ever stop feeling guilty?

Chapter 9

The day dawned with drizzle. Kat felt it was appropriate. The sky would be crying along with all the people who really knew and cared for Amber. Maybe some of her classmates would stay away. Who wants to stand in the rain and watch a casket being lowered into the ground? She sure didn't, but she would go. She owed it to Amber and to her mom.

Kat liked Sheila. She seemed like she was trying hard to keep things together. First, she lost her husband and had to downsize her lifestyle and Amber's. She worked a decent job, but there were no frills. Now this.

She hauled herself out of bed, took a shower, and got ready to go with her mom to the funeral home. Sheila had asked them to come as family. She grabbed a bagel and slathered it with cream cheese as she picked up the mug of coffee her mom set out for her. Kat dreaded the day to come. Stupid chit-chat with her friends. The meal someone was serving after. Making people think she and Amber had been real friends. She was the fake. At least her friends admitted they didn't know her well.

Silently her mom drove to Sheila's. Kat thought they were going to the funeral home. She was surprised to learn they would be riding with Sheila in the limo following the hearse. It made her shudder. She knew there would be no riding with friends and maybe it wasn't all bad.

They were led in a private door at the funeral home. Angela and Kat were seated with Sheila in the front row for family, the next three rows were taken up by Sheila's family and her husband's family. After they were seated, the classmates, teachers, and counselors were seated. Then, it was anyone left over. Including some plain clothes police officers.

The minister talked about what a wonderful young girl Amber had been. At some point, while listening to him, Kat realized he'd never met Amber. He was reading things others had told him about her. She felt like this was another sham and she couldn't wait to get it done. The eulogy was given by one of Amber's cousins. Finally, someone who really knew Amber. She shared happy memories of their growing up and how when Amber moved they grew apart. When she cried, Kat knew they were genuine tears and admired the girl for them.

After the funeral, they went to the gravesite for the service there. Kat was amazed at how many people came. The drizzle continued, and umbrellas were everywhere. When it was over, people loaded back in their cars and went to a local restaurant who donated food and a private room for the meal.

There was little talk as people ate. After the meal was served, people moved around the room talking to family and friends. Sheila kept Kat and Angela at her side. She introduced them as family friends. Kat realized, Angela had been so busy starting a new life, she hadn't had time to make any friends of her own. She had co-workers many of whom had showed up at the funeral, but not at the dinner. Finally, guests started leaving. Kat was relieved she had dodged most of her friends. While they came to Sheila to offer condolences, they did not linger to talk to Kat.

When they got back to Sheila's it felt like a haven against a storm. Angela helped Sheila with leftover dishes and then Sheila went to lie down. Kat and Angela left.

In their apartment, Kat collapsed on the sofa. “I’m glad it’s over.”

“I saw a lot of kids there today. I think it was a good sign,” Angela responded.

“A sign they were able to skip class, and no one would mark it down,” Kat sneered.

“Why do you feel like this?” Angela’s concern was evident.

“It’s just no one made an effort to really know her. The only person who was genuinely sad was the girl who gave the eulogy,” Kat responded. “I really hate the questions some of my friends are asking. Take Max, he wanted to know if I’d seen Amber at the hospital. When I told him yes, he asked if it was gross. It wasn’t gross, it was devastating watching the end of a person’s life.” Tears of frustration ran down her face. The first tears she had cried.

Angela went to her side, “Oh, Baby. It’s hard to lose someone you know even if it’s only casually. We all react to death differently. Maybe Max has never seen anyone die. Maybe he is afraid.”

“But I feel so guilty,” Kat sobbed. “I should have done more.”

“We always feel guilty. It’s part of our grief. I don’t think you could have done more. You walked with her and worked with her in tutoring. You didn’t have to be her best friend to care.”

“I guess, but it still feels awful. Like there is something I should be doing.”

“You’ll figure it out. Why don’t you go lie down?”

Kat stood, “Thanks, Mom.” Then she walked to her room. She changed out of her funeral clothes and pulled on some sweats. She turned her phone on only to find it filled with messages. She didn’t want to read them now, so she turned the phone off again. She laid down on the bed and was soon asleep.

Chapter 10

Kat went through school in a fog. She was aware of giving answers when called on in class. She listened to her friends talk but, didn't contribute to the conversations. As promised, Officer Madi Jones was waiting for her when school let out.

They walked to the coffee shop. Madi trying to keep up a running conversation.

"So, tell me about your day," she prompted.

"It was okay, I guess," Kat replied. "I've kinda been in a fog."

"Understandable, but if we're going to convince this guy I'm a friend, you're going to have to be more involved."

"I'll try," Kat replied. "Hey, how do you feel about the upcoming Sadie Hawkins Dance?"

"They still have those?" Madi was shocked. "I thought they went out with feminism."

"Yep, we get to ask the guy of our dreams," was Kat's sarcastic reply.

"I take it you don't buy into it."

"Nope, don't want to be humiliated by asking someone and having him turn me down."

"Why on earth would anyone turn you down? You're beautiful."

"Ha!" Kat snorted. "Beauty is in the eye of the beholder. Guys are looking for a girl who will put out. It's not me."

"There must be someone who doesn't feel like that," Madi insisted.

"Let me know if you find him. Otherwise, I will continue to be known as the Ice Princess."

"They really call you that?"

"So, I've heard," Kat replied. "It used to bother me, but not so much anymore. I want to be liked for my brain as much as my looks."

"Good girl, you hold out for someone who does," Madi approved.

When they reached the coffee shop, they joined Kat's friends. "This is Madi Jones, she's thinking of transferring to our school. I told her to come hang out with us here."

As if on cue the girls said, "Welcome, Madi."

"I'm Trix, what are you interested in?"

"You mean besides guys?" Madi laughed. "I'm into horticulture."

"Horti-who?" Sam asked.

"Growing plants," Madi explained. "Like herb gardens and flowers. We used to have a roof top garden, but we had to move. I miss it."

"Are you a vegetarian or vegan?" Trix wanted to know.

"Nope, but I do like vegetables and herbs," Madi replied. "I just want to leave a smaller carbon footprint."

Nodding her head Sam said, "I get it now. You're into the environmental thing."

"Sort of," Madi replied. "It's a way to be good to the environment and fiscally responsible."

"You sure use big words," Trix commented. "My dad uses the term fiscally responsible when talking to my mom about her spending habits."

"I'm going to need money for college," Madi said. "I won't get enough in scholarships to pay for everything. It's part of why I want to transfer here. It's a better school than where I'm at."

"Wow," Sam said. "I just count on my parents to pay for college."

"My mom will help, but with two younger kids and my dad skipped town, I'm going to have to pull my own weight," Madi explained.

"Sorry to hear about your dad," Kat said. "My parents are divorced, but the one thing they did was set up a college fund for my brother and I, so we wouldn't have to worry about student loans."

Kat looked up then nudged Madi under the table. Madi looked at her and Kat nodded toward the door. Sure, enough there stood the man who had killed Amber.

"Hey, will one of you point me to the ladies' room?" Madi asked.

"Just down the hall behind you, first door on the right," Sam said.

Madi stood and walked to the ladies' room. Inside she pulled out her cell phone and texted her partner who was in a van outside.

Madi: Perp inside

Wells: Teams coming

Madi: Roger

She walked back to the table and sat down. "So, who's going to the Sadie Hawkins dance?"

Before anyone could answer cops came from the back and in through the front door. "Police, hands on your head, Rivera."

The man Kat thought of as the creep turned to see the officers, "What seems to be the problem, Officer?"

"Hands on your head, *now*!"

Rivera complied by putting his hands on his head.

"Now on your knees."

Rivera dropped to his knees.

A different officer walked up behind him and hand cuffed him behind his back.

"Anton Rivera, you are under arrest for kidnapping and murder. You have the right to remain silent. Anything you say can and will be used against you in a court of law. You have the right to an attorney, if you cannot afford one, the court will appoint you an attorney. Do you understand these rights as I've read them to you?"

"I do. I have my own attorney."

"Good you can call him from the precinct."

Without any further commotion, they led the man out an put him in a squad car. The cars all drove away.

"What was that all about?" Trix wanted to know? "That guy is always in here after school. He gives me the creeps."

"Have any of you talked to him before," Madi asked.

"Nope, he's the reason we never leave alone," Sam said.

Trix said, "I wonder who he kidnapped and murdered?"

"Think about it, Trix," Kat said disgustedly.

"You know!" Trix was incredulous.

Kat just shook her head. "How can you be smart and be so stupid?"

"Oh, my God!" Sam exclaimed. "He killed Amber. I saw him as a person of interest on TV."

"Hey, Gals, I think we should all go home now," Madi suggested. "My friend, Bobby has a van outside. We'll drop you off at your houses."

"Great idea," Kat said.

The girls gathered their things and headed out to Bobby's van. Bobby was a young officer who looked like he was still in high school. The girls piled in and they left to take them all home.

Kat was the last to get home. Madi looked at her and said, "You did great today."

"Thanks," Kat said and smiled for the first time in days.

"Reconsider the dance, you might have fun," Madi suggested.

"I might. And thanks," Kat replied.

Madi walked her to the front door of the apartment building. She handed Kat her card. "If there is ever anything, or you just need to talk. Call me." She hugged Kat and watched her go inside, then went down to join Bobby in the van.

The arrest of Anton Rivera was Breaking News on all the channels at six o'clock. Kat watched with her mom and brother. She felt like she'd done some good. Officer Madi turned out to be a good decoy. The trial was still to come, but other girls were safe for now. That night for the first time since Amber disappeared, Kat had a good night's sleep.

The Unused Crib

Dedicated to:
The memory of those who gave their all

The sign hung on an angle looking as forlorn as the words is carried:

For Sale
Baby Crib Never Used

I looked at the sign and the ramshackled house behind it, wondering what tragedy had occurred. *Had the baby been stillborn? Did the mother miscarry? Had there been an accident?* I slowly approached the house to see if the crib was still available.

An ancient woman about four feet tall answered my knock. "I came to see the crib."

"Come in." She ushered me into her dark and shabby home. "This way."

She opened a door. In the center of the room was a handmade cradle.

"Why wasn't it used? It's so beautiful!" the words escaped from my mouth.

"My husband built it, then went off to serve in the war. He was on the beach at Normandy," she said with pride. "He's buried in Arlington."

At a loss for words, I just asked, "How much?"

"Whatever you can spare, child," the woman answered.

In my purse was $250 I had planned to spend for an entire bedroom set for the baby. I reached in and took out the envelope from the bank. "Will this be enough?"

Taking the envelope, the little woman smiled through her tears and said, "Bless you child and the babe you carry."

We carried the cradle to my van and I thanked her again.

When my son was born, I went to look for the woman. There was a sign in her front yard

For Sale

I called the realtor to inquire about the former owner of the house.

The polite lady on the line said, "I'm sorry Mrs. Wesley died. She wanted the proceeds to go to the local veterans as she had no living relatives. But she did ask if anyone should inquire, we let them know the purchase of a baby crib paid for the rest of her funeral. I'm sorry I don't know what that means."

Smiling I said, "I do. Do you happen to know where she is buried? Also, did she ever mention her husband's name?"

"She's in the Oak Lawn Cemetery on the edge of town. The care taker there can lead you to the grave site. I believe her husband's name was William."

"Thank you," I told her. Hanging up the phone I cried. I had named my son, William. It must be an omen. Later I would go to the cemetery and lay flowers on her grave. I think it would be nice to talk to her again.

The Heir

Chapter 1

I awoke slowly aware I was not in my bedroom. My head ached as I took in my surroundings, I noticed the bars. How did I end up in jail? I sat up slowly holding my head, unable to remember what happened last night.

I stood reaching into my pocket for a stick of gum, anything to take this horrible taste from my mouth. Pulling out my hand I found five things.

First, was a book of matches. I turned them over slowly and read the name on the package, *Escape Gentlemen's Club*. What on earth was I doing with these? I'm not a smoker. Why had I been there? Was it a case?

Next was a napkin, it too had the emblem of *Escape* and a number. It wasn't a phone number-there weren't enough numbers. This was becoming a puzzle.

There was also a key, not a car key. Motels use key cards, so not from one of those. When I turned it over, "Bank of Michigan" was imprinted on it. This might be a safe deposit box key, but I didn't have a safety deposit box.

Item number four looked like a worm. Oh, heavens, the worm from a tequila bottle. I never ate those. How did it get into my pocket? Disgusting! I shivered.

The last item was a business card. It belonged to a person named Jesse Barstow. Who was this person? Why did I have his card? Was he a client?

I sat on the bunk and tried to put my thoughts in order. That's when the officer showed up.

"Come with me. We're serving breakfast before we turn you loose."

I followed quietly pondering the items in my pocket. I was put in a small conference room. Coffee and donuts were on a counter along one wall.

"Go ahead, help yourself. The chief will be here in a minute."

I took a cup of coffee, added a ton of sugar, and a bit of milk. Then, took a jelly donut from the box. I just started on the donut when the chief walked in.

"Well, Sam, you got yourself into it this time, didn't you?"

"I would like to agree with you, Chief, but I'm not sure what happened last night."

"Let me see if I can fill in some of the blanks. One of my officers found you wandering down the street at one o'clock in the morning. He recognized you and brought you here. You seemed to be in some kind of state and were non-responsive to questions. I told them to take a blood sample and run it for toxins. Someone slipped you Rohypnol-the date rape drug. I immediately had them take you to ER. They ran a rape kit, but it came back negative. Someone was trying to put you out of business, Sam. What do you remember?"

I reached into my pocket and pulled out the five items. Things started to fall into place. I was hired by Jesse Barstow to find someone. He met me at *Escape*, where I picked up the matchbook. The key and the napkin were still a bit of a mystery. I could not explain the worm.

I explained what I could to the chief. We looked at the key and the number on the napkin. He took the business card.

As I sat there finishing my coffee, I went for another donut. There was still a big blank. *Why didn't they keep me at the hospital?* Being a private investigator, the police department held me in as much esteem as they would a pile of dung. But, I had paid my dues in the department and it counted for something.

The chief came back as I was finishing the second donut. He shook his head, "Beats me how you can eat that stuff and still be thin as a rail. I ran a check on this Jesses Barstow. Seems he has a yellow sheet longer than your arm. He's quite the con man. I can't believe you fell for him."

"I'm not sure I did. He might the person who drugged me. I went to *Escape* looking for Molly Marshfield. The key belongs to her. It was for her mother's safe deposit box. I just can't remember the numbers and what they were about."

"Barstow just approached you?"

"No, he called earlier in the day. He wanted me to find someone for him. Since I had to go see Molly, I told him to meet me at *Escape.*"

"He identified himself by giving you his card? Had you already talked to Molly?"

"She was finishing up a set. I have not talked to her; I still have the key."

"Were you writing on the napkin?"

"I don't remember. I don't know how I got it or what it was about." I shook my head hoping to bring back the memory.

"Well, you seem to be okay now. I didn't want to send you home last night if you were facing some kind of danger. I've put out a BOLO (Be on the Lookout) for Barstow. I have some questions for him. Want a lift to your place?" the chief asked.

"Thanks, Dad, but if it's all the same to you, I'd like to go see Mom."

"We should both go, Kiddo, give me a minute and we'll be off."

Yeah, my dad is the Chief of Police. We try to see Mom two or three times a week. She has Alzheimer's and lives in a local nursing home. Sometimes it's easier if we both go together. I was ready when Dad came back.

Chapter 2

We drove to the nursing home in silence. I knew he disliked my choice of career. He disliked it when I was a police officer, too. In his opinion. it was not a job for a girl…especially not *his* little girl.

"Dad. The napkin, it's an address," I said out of the blue.

"An address to what?"

"The address to the nursing home and it includes Mom's room number," I urgently replied.

Instantly, lights and sirens were on. We flew through town. I was out of the car and running before Dad could come to a complete stop. Nurses and administrators were coming out the front door to see what the commotion was. I bowled past them headed for Mom's room. She looked up as I entered.

"Samantha, dear have you been running again? You know it's not ladylike," she admonished like a thousand other times in my life.

"I know, Mom." I stopped a minute to take in her surroundings. Nothing seemed out of place.

Dad came in a moment later. He smiled at Mom and asked, "How are you, Helen?"

"I'm fine. What is all the commotion about?" she asked with a puzzled expression on her face.

"Mom, have you had any visitors?" I was in full interrogation mode.

"Why, yes. A young man from the church came in and left his card." She handed it to me. Sure enough it was Jesse Barstow. I gave it to Dad.

"We were just worried about you, Mom," I told her my hand going to her snow white hair in a caress.

"I'm fine. These people take good care of me," she said a serene smile on her face.

Dad stepped over to her. "Helen we were just concerned. We have to leave now, but we'll be back later." He kissed her and walked out of the room.

"I'm so glad you and your dad are getting along again."

"Bye, Mom, love you." I kissed her on the cheek and followed Dad.

When we got into the car, he said, "Sam, will you stay with me until we find this guy?"

"Normally, I'd say no, but this guy found Mom."

"Good girl. I think I know what the key is to. This is not Molly's key," he said seriously.

"How do you know?" My turn to be puzzled.

"I received a call after you got out of the car. Molly got her key last night. She said you left with some guy."

"This is the key to your mother's safety deposit box. I had them check the bank and find out who the key belonged to. I want to go and see if he got into it."

"I'm going with you." I looked him in the eye letting him know I was ready to argue.

"You bet you are. You have power of attorney for this box," he said simply gaining the upper hand.

"Oh, Dad, no, you don't think he stole from the box, do you?" My brows drew together indicating I was worried.

"I think because you still have the key, things are okay," was his reassuring response.

We drove to the bank, talked to the manager, and went to get the safety deposit box. Nothing was unusual. It held my grandmother's jewelry and some savings bonds my mother had for me.

With help from the bank manager, the box was changed and a new key was issued. The chief drove me to my apartment, I threw some clothing in a bag, and he took me home. I went upstairs took a long shower and changed. When I came down there were two officers in the living room. I knew them both. Anna Wilkins, petite and good-natured was assigned to the house. Jack Adams tall, lanky, with a desire to please was going to be in the car outside.

I went up to my old room, crawled between the sheets, and was asleep in minutes.

The chief went back to the office to check on the status of the BOLO and finish up his day. He called the administrator of the nursing home. He wanted no visitors in his wife's room not personally known to the staff. A man who claimed to be from the church had shown up today, and he was not welcome. Once he had taken care of the nursing home, he turned his attention to finding Barstow…and learn what his game was.

Chapter 3

Later in the day, I awoke, felt refreshed, dressed, and wandered downstairs to find something to eat. I found Anna in the kitchen and wonderful aromas wafting out.

"Afternoon, Sam, hope you don't mind me taking over the kitchen. The chief will be home in about half an hour. If you can wait that long, I'll have dinner for you."

"Anna, that's great!! Can't wait," I told her.

She reached into the fridge and grabbed a bottle of water. She handed it to me and I sat at the counter.

"So, did you get drafted to go to ER with me last night?" I asked.

"I volunteered," she replied with a smile.

"Thanks. I wish I could remember. I don't even recall seeing Molly," I said morosely.

"I talked to Molly today. She came to see you when her set was done. When she did, you weren't to coherent. You gave her the key and told her what it was for. She said you weren't too steady on your feet."

Shrugging, I drank some water. Something was nagging at me. I knew it would be important. Try as I might, I could not grab onto it.

When the chief arrived, Anna put dinner on the table. I asked Anna to stay, but she said she needed to get home to her husband. She left and we sat down to dinner.

"Dad, there's something in the back of my mind about last night. I can't seem to hang onto it long enough to remember."

"It'll come to you. Don't think about it now," he said calmly.

"Do we have night coverage, too? Maybe we should take them some of this delicious pork," I said trying to figure out how serious this situation was.

"No one is assigned to watch the house tonight. They are doing a drive-by every half hour."

"Thanks, Dad." I meant it and smiled.

"Just a precaution. I took care of your mother, too," he told me.

I nodded and continued to eat my dinner. After dinner, Dad and I took coffee in the den. We watched some TV together before I went up to bed.

My sleep was restless, filled with images running into each other. Jesse Barstow kept running through my head. *What had he wanted me to do? Why had he hired me? Why had he drugged me? How did my mother fit in?* I woke tired and still drawing a blank.

Dad had coffee on when I came downstairs. He was just putting bacon in the pan. Looking up he asked, "Couldn't sleep either?"

"Nope, still cannot get to the niggling little thing in my head."

" It'll come to you. What have you got; you have to be working on?" he questioned.

"I just finished up for Molly, so the job offer from Barstow would have been the next thing. I'm going to call and see if I have any messages." Going to the phone I called my office and checked my voice mail. I received a cryptic message from Barstow.

So, you are a hotshot PI? I don't think so. You fell for the oldest con in the book. It was easy to get you where I wanted you.

I replayed it so Dad could listen. He sent Anna over to get the tape and have it analyzed.

Then, I called my home to check the for any voice mail there. Surprisingly there were none. I was careful not to give it out to my clients. My office and cell phones were for business.

Dad and I ate in silence. I cleaned up after breakfast while Dad went to get ready for work.

Anna showed up as Dad came down the stairs. He nodded to me and said to both of us, "You girls keep out of trouble." Then he left.

Chapter 4

I poured a second cup of coffee and offered a cup to Anna. We sat in the living room.

"So, what big plans do we have for the day? I brought my own car so we'd be less conspicuous if went out." She was always eager to help.

"I don't know. Maybe web surf on Dad's computer. I may be able to remote access my files. I need to know what Barstow wanted to hire me for. Maybe then I will know what it is I can't remember."

"Need any help? I'm pretty good at hacking into systems," she volunteered.

I looked at her wide-eyed. "You're not serious."

"Sure, I took training at Quantico on how to hack into systems. I have a computer background."

We went to Dad's office, I booted up the computer and typed in my website and logged in. I went to the section I kept on potential clients. Then I opened the file I'd started on Barstow. Anna and I quickly read through my notes. Nothing seemed out of the ordinary. He wanted me to find his missing daughter. He lost track of her after he divorced her mother. We agreed to meet.

"Did he email you a photo?" she asked.

"I don't remember."

Excitedly she said, "Here, let me look."

I slid off the chair and let Anna sit down, then pulled another chair alongside her. She typed quickly and accessed my photos. Sure enough there was a file labeled Barstow. I was almost afraid to look. When the picture came up, I was floored. The picture was of me taken at the beach about ten years ago. *How did he come to have this photo? Who is this man?*

Anna looked at me speechless. I think my expression mirrored hers. I reached for the phone and called the police department.

"Applewood Police Department, how may I direct you?"

"Agnes, this is Sam. Is my dad in yet?"

"He's just walking through the door. Hold on a minute."

The next voice I heard was Dad's, "What's up?"

"I need you to come home. Anna and I found something on the computer you need to see." The seriousness of my voice had him on alert.

"Want to tell me about it?" he asked.

"No, Dad, I need you here," I told him.

"Okay, I'll be there in ten minutes." The next thing I heard was the dial tone.

Anna printed the photo. She wanted to have a hard copy when Dad got there. She also saved the photo to a disk. We shut the computer down and went to wait.

When Dad came in a few minutes later, I handed him the photo. He looked at it questioningly.

"Barstow wanted me to find his daughter. He sent me a ten year old picture of her. Dad, who is this guy and why does he think I'm his daughter?" I wanted to know.

Dad just sat and looked at me. I could see he was measuring what he wanted to say. I waited. Anna left the room presumably to give us some privacy.

Chapter 5

"He may be your biological father. Your mother was pregnant when I married her.

The guy had run off. I didn't care. I loved your mother. Her child would be mine. We were never able to have other children and I figured it was my fault. This man Barstow, which is not his real name, is looking for an heir. He is Allen Bannister, Jr. and once he produces one, he will inherit a trust worth millions. But the money is tied up waiting on an heir. The trust will be divided equally between the heir and Bannister."

"Dad, I'm not his heir. I'm your daughter and Mom's. Take a good look at me. I'm five-five just like Mom and you are always telling me I have her eyes. I have your blond hair and coloring. Nothing will change." I was furious.

"He's going to want a DNA test," Dad stated.

"Let's do one," I demanded.

"Are you sure?" He raised his eyebrows.

"Yes, I'm positive. Was Mom pregnant when you met her or when you got married?" I asked.

"I never really thought about it," he answered honestly. "I knew she'd been thrown over by this guy. Ours was a whirlwind romance. I wasn't even sure she loved me at first."

"Anna, we're going to see the ME (medical examiner), care to come along," I yelled.

She appeared nodding her head, yes. The three of us left. Anna following in her car. It took no time to reach the medical examiner's office.

Doc Watson was quick to take cheek swabs. He told us it would be a few weeks, but he'd put a rush on it. In the meantime, Anna and I were going back to the house. I want to know everything I could about the man I knew as Barstow.

We arrived at home, Anna threw together some sandwiches, grabbed a couple bottles of water, and booted up the computer. We started with a people search of Allen Bannister, Jr. Once we got a photo of him, we went on to search his family. A quick credit card to Intellus and we had a fountain of information. Bannister was the family bad boy. He had a sister who was a lawyer, a brother who was a doctor, and he seemed to be the wastrel. I couldn't see where he had ever finished college, but he had attended four different universities. He hadn't held a job for over a year. We found a couple of tickets for DUI-driving under the influence. He had some gambling debts. It appears a couple of incident with women were hushed. Apparently, he had no children. I didn't want this man to be my father. I didn't want his money or his name.

I left the room frustrated. Anna printed off all the information we found. She also found an empty file folder and put the it in there. Slowly she followed me to the kitchen.

"Sam, what do you want to do with this?" she asked waving the folder.

"Frankly, I want to burn it. I want nothing to do with this man, especially after last night. What kind of father give his daughter Rohypnol and leaves her wandering on the side of the road?" I could feel the anger burning inside me.

"I don't know. Not a good one for sure," Anna agreed.

"He can't be my dad, Anna, he just can't. Why my mother didn't even recognize him."

"She has Alzheimer's. She has days when she doesn't recognize you. Doesn't she?" Anna probed.

"Not yet. She's been pretty lucid on the days Dad and I go to visit her."

"This man would be a stranger. Not someone she has seen in recent years," she reminded me.

"How'd he get that photograph of me? I remember being at the beach. I was with a bunch of school friends. I don't remember anyone taking pictures of me." I was like a caged lion now.

"Any good investigator can take photos from long distance. You know that. You've gotten some shots which have helped us when we couldn't get close."

"Yeah, I suppose. This is just so disturbing." I don't know what was more frustrating, that this man *could* be me father or, that he thought so little of me, drugging me, and leaving me alone unprotected.

"The chief will find him. Then we'll get to the bottom of all this," Anna tried to be reassuring.

"I suppose. Well, we better make a plan for the next couple of weeks. We are going to be together a lot."

Anna laughed. "I guess you're right. What sounds like fun?"

Chapter 6

We spent the next two weeks hacking into every file holding information on Allen Bannister, Jr. We learned he was broke and owe money to some online gambling establishments. He appeared to live the high life and treated people badly. His scrapes with the law always managed to go away. It appeared as though his lawyer sister got the charges dropped or his wealthy father must have put large sums of money out to make them disappear. When Dad called to say, Doc Watson had DNA results, I felt armed to battle this man who claimed to be my father. We had an appointment with Doc Watson in the morning.

I tossed and turned all night. I was up early, showered, dressed, and making breakfast when Dad came down the stairs. I poured him a cup of coffee and he sat at the counter. When I had breakfast on plates, we moved to the table.

"I heard you roaming around last night. Are you sure you want to go with me?" he asked concerned.

"Yes, Dad, I want this over one way or the other. With Anna's help I have enough information on this man to make him go away. Not to mention he left *ME* on the side of the road drugged."

We finished breakfast in silence and I did the dishes. Then we headed to the car and drove to the ME's office. Doc was waiting for us and took us right in.

"I don't mean to keep you in suspense, but I need to know why you wanted this test," his demeanor said it shouldn't be an issue.

"There's a man out there claiming to be my biological father and he wants to destroy my life and family," I retorted hotly.

"Well, I don't know who this guy is, but he's barking up the wrong tree. I won't ask Chief, but I can't imagine you needed a test to know this high spirited young woman is your daughter. I did run the DNA an voila the results are as I suspected…Samantha is your daughter."

I could hardly contain myself. I threw my arms around Dad. "Well, this has paid off, we can now add kidnapping to the charges against him," I beamed.

The chief's phone rang at that moment. "Excuse me," he said as he stood up to walk across the room. "This is the chief. Uh-hu. Okay. I'll tell her. Thanks."

"Sam, they picked up Bannister. Would you like to be the one to tell him he doesn't have an heir?"

"You bet." I turned to Doc and gave him a big hug, too. "Thanks, so much."

He handed me the file with the DNA report. Dad shook his hand and we walked out. The ride to the police department didn't take long. They told Dad Bannister was in an interrogation room. We walked in together father *and* daughter.

Chapter 7

"Mr. Bannister, imagine you here and under arrest," I said sarcastically.

"What is she doing here? I asked for a lawyer. I want her out of here," he demanded.

"Well now, what you want doesn't much matter. A public defender has been called until your lawyer can get here. I just thought I'd let Sam read the list of charges," the chief replied.

"She can't! She's a civilian. She has no right to be in this room," he raged.

"Wrong, Scumbag, I have every right to be here. You are first being charged with kidnapping, then there is the issue of the Rohypnol, finally there is the charge of impersonation." I was enjoying this.

"You misled me. You advertise as a private investigator," he complained.

"I *am* a private investigator. I'm also the daughter of the chief of police. Which was your first mistake," I informed him.

"You're my daughter. I hired someone to find you," he argued back.

"Taking photos of me does not make me your daughter. The DNA test in my hand says otherwise," I smirked as I held up the folder Doc had given me.

"I didn't have a DNA test done. Those results must be forged," he said defiantly.

"I had one done with *my* father. Those tests are correct. You aren't my father. This is a good thing because I have a file on you which will bury you in some stinking jail cell for a great number of years. You'll probably be to old to father an heir when you see the outside again."

"I have no idea what you are talking about. I want this woman out of here. I also want a private DNA test done. She is my daughter," Bannister continued to insist looking at the chief.

I turned and walked out, too angry with this spoiled rich man to care. I passed the public defender on his way to the interrogation room. I went to the conference room. In a couple of minutes, Anna joined me.

"So, how's it going?" care and concern filling her voice.

"I have a DNA test saying the scumbag is not related to me. I should be happy. Instead, I want to bury him in a jail cell for a long, long time." Shrugging I tossed the file on the table.

"It will take time, Sam. This man wanted you to be someone you're not. It's hard to take." Anna's presence was comforting.

"I know in my head you're right, but my heart is angry." I had trouble letting go of my rage.

"Give it time. His arraignment is scheduled for 1 pm. Will you be there?" Anna asked.

"Yes, I need to talk to Dad. Then I'm going home." I could feel the rage start to seep out, leaving me tired.

"Let me know if you need a lift." She smiled and headed for the door.

"Thanks, Anna for everything." I returned her smile.

"No problem. Its' just part of the *protect and serve*." She left me and went back to her job. The chief found me sitting at the table.

"Sam, are you okay," he wanted to know.

"Yeah, Dad, I'm just angry." I looked at him to see if my anger was reflected there.

"Let's get some lunch and we'll go to the arraignment together," he suggested.

I nodded and we left. Lunch was a quiet affair at a little grill up the street from the police station.

After we ordered Dad said, "I'm sorry we had to do the DNA test. Your mother is a good woman. She would never have wanted you to know there was a chance you were not mine."

"It's a dead issue. I'm yours. DNA is not what bothers me. I'm afraid he'll make bail and I won't be safe." I looked at Dad, rarely did I let him see my fear.

"I will keep a patrol going by your place or you can continue staying with me. We have the District Attorney on board with all the information you and Anna dug up, he has a lot to answer for. Anna's name is on it so it won't be considered tainted. You are just the victim. He will not be offered bail, because he has no ties to the community and is a flight risk," he answered with confidence.

"I hope you're right."

Chapter 8

Our order came and we ate. Then we drove to the courthouse. The courtroom was filled with old wood making you feel almost reverent when you entered. We sat in the courtroom and listened to the District Attorney give reasons why Bannister should be remanded to custody. His court appointed lawyer did not object. Bannister was fuming at the remand. He knew he would have to wait a while for his sister to arrive.

Dad and I left the courthouse in silence. He dropped me off at my apartment and we made plans to visit Mom tomorrow.

The trial went on for five days. Bannister's slick sister, the lawyer, was defending him. The surprise was Allen Bannister, Sr, sitting there every day. The white-haired man sat erectly as he heard every word describing his worthless son. On the day the case went to the jury, he approached me.

"Miss Worth?"

"Yes."

"I am Allen Bannister, Sr. I'd like a moment of your time," he said softly.

Stunned I responded, "I don't think we have anything to talk about."

"You *may* change your mind, when you hear what I have to say. I have a proposition for you," he continued as if I'd said nothing.

Thinking it would hurt to hear what he had to say, I said, "This way."

We walked out of the courtroom to an unoccupied conference room. I sat and waited for him to speak.

“First, I want to say how sorry I am for what my son has done to you. He has always been a disappointment. Second, I would like to thank you for the thorough job you did investigating him. There are many things about him I did not know. Finally, *I* have a trust fund to disperse.”

“I’m not sure how that affects me,” I said hesitantly.

“That is what I wanted to talk to you about. You are, too intelligent to have been my son’s child. I understand he besmirched your mother’s reputation and caused untold hurt to you and your father. I’d like to take his half of the fund and put it into an account to take care of your mother to the end of her life. On her death, the remainder will go to your father. The rest, I would like you to have.”

“You don’t need to give us money,” I responded hotly thinking this man was trying to buy me off.

“I know I don’t, but I have no other children and I’d like something good to come of this. For my part, I’d like to know if I need an investigator in the future, I can call on you. I would be honored if you would accept this.”

“May I have time to think about it?” I asked.

“You may have until the jury returns with a verdict,” he replied.

“Thank you.” I put out my hand and he shook it. Then he left the room.

I talked to Dad about this over dinner. He as adamant at first, he wanted no blood money from the Bannisters. I told him to sleep on it. We could talk in the morning.

Chapter 9

At breakfast, Dad was quiet. Then he said, "The money would come in handy for helping your mom."

"I know, Dad. I thought so, too. It will also help if something should happen to you."

"I don't know what you have decided, but for my part, you can tell Bannister I'm good with it."

"I've thought long and hard. If there is money left, when you and Mom are both gone, I'll use the money for two things; one to improve the local library and one will be to fund Alzheimer's research."

Dad said, "I'd like to add a third."

"What would it be?" I asked.

"I'd like a scholarship at the school in your mom's name," he answered quietly.

"It's something we could do. I'll talk to Bannister today and have him draw up the papers," I told him.

Bannister agreed and his daughter drew up the papers. I signed them and we went into the courtroom to hear the verdict.

Allen Bannister, Jr was found guilty of kidnapping and possession of a date rape drug. He was sentenced to twenty-five years to life. Life for Dad and I went back to normal. Me…I was just hoping *never* to wake up in a jail cell again.

The End

Broken Chains

For my mom, Donavee Vigus

Chapter 1

The Holler was the last place Dixie wanted to be, juke box blaring, the smell of cigarettes, and the sweat of the drunks who grabbed at her as she served them. Tonight was her night off, except one of the girls called in, and the boss knew he could count on Dixie to cover the shift because she need the money.

Dixie hated the job; however as a single mom of two, she needed the decent pay and good tips. Her fifteen-year-old sister, Ellen Jean, baby-sat which helped. Dixie knew her kids were well taken care of and also knew where to find Ellen Jean. She felt she'd been raising kids all her life. As the eldest of seven when her parent died in a car accident, it fell to Dixie and John Jr to bring up the younger ones. Junior had just graduated high school and Dixie was home after her first year of college. She stayed home and Junior gave up his dream of college to keep the kids together. Everyone pitched in to keep the farm running. That was ten years ago.

"Hey, Dixie, honey! When you going to cave in and go out with me?" Hank yelled above the music.

"I don't date customers, Hank," she quipped on her way to the bar for refills.

Hank winked and reached for her as she returned. "I know you're lonely for me," he said slyly.

Dixie set the drinks on the table and said, "You keep dreamin'."

As she turned to walk away, Hank grabbed her from behind and pulled her on his lap. Dixie was mad at herself for not realizing how drunk he was.

"Gimme a kiss, Honey," he pleaded drunkenly.

Trapped, Dixie twisted and pressed the heel of her shoe into Hank's foot. He howled like a wounded animal and let her go. She stood, put distance between them, and glared at the angry man.

"I'm sorry, Hank; but you know the rules. No sittin' with the customers." She stalked away.

She stood at the bar waiting for orders for another table to be filled, "Better close, Hank's tab, Tom. He's going to have trouble walking out of here much less driving."

Tom nodded and finished filling the drink order. He closed out the tab and signaled to Donna, the other waitress to collect. He shook his head as he looked at Hank. *No sense having him make another scene over Dixie.*

The rest of the shift went without incident. Dixie was glad when the juke box stopped playing and the lights went out. There were only two customers left and Tom shooed them out.

Dixie grabbed a tub from the kitchen and went back to start bussing, cleaning tables, and stacking chairs on them when she finished each one. It did not take long. Donna had started in the front and they met in the middle. Dixie took the last of the dishes to the kitchen. Donna went to the storage room for the broom and mop pail.

They worked as a team. Dixie went through sweeping the floor and Donna followed her with the mop. When they finished, they put everything away, collected their tip jars and clocked out.

Dixie was tired and ready for bed but woke instantly at the sight of four slashed tires. She ran her hands through her strawberry-blonde hair thinking, *What next?*

"Who on earth would have done this?" she asked no one in particular.

"Maybe it was Hank. You did step on his foot," Donna suggested.

"I doubt it," Dixie said. "He had to be carried out. See," she said pointing, "his car is still here."

"Dixie," Tom yelled from the door. "Let me take you home and we'll get it fixed tomorrow."

Resigned, Dixie followed him to his truck. "I live over on Oak Street. The little house on the turn around," she said climbing in.

"I know. Let's get you home."

A few minutes later they were in her driveway. Tom parked, got out, rounded the truck, opened Dixie's door, and started to walk her to the door.

"I appreciate the ride, Tom, but I can make it to the door by myself," she said softly.

"I reckon you can. I just don't want anyone waiting to grab you," he responded.

"Ok, thanks," she said a bit chagrinned assuming Tom wanted something more.

Dixie took out her key, before putting the key in she turned to thank Tom again. He stood silently at the bottom of the porch steps.

"Lock up tight when you get in. I'll stop by the sheriff's office and let them know you had trouble. Night, Dixie." He turned to leave.

"Tom."

He turned, smiled at her, and said, "Weren't nothin', Kid." The he walked to his truck, opened the door, and climbed in.

Once inside, Dixie locked the door watched from the window as Tom drove away, then turned off the porch light. She hung her coat on the rack, took off her shoes, and headed down the hall to the bathroom. After showering the smell of the bar way, she tip-toed in to check on her kids, Lacy and Dustin, who were both sound asleep. She bent down to kiss each one on the forehead. Next, she peeked in on Ellen Jean, who was sound asleep clutching a stuffed bear from her latest beau. Dixie covered her with a blanket and kissed her forehead.

She made her way to her room, tumbled into bed, and was instantly asleep.

Chapter 2

Dixies awoke to silence. She looked at the clock next to her bed...seven-thirty. Where were the children? They should be getting ready for church. Quickly she got up, threw on her robe, opened the door, and stopped. Wonderful smells wafted to her from the kitchen and she heard snippets of conversation.

"Is it almost done?" Dustin's anxious whisper carried down the hall.

"Almost," Lacey hissed.

"It's ready," Ellen Jean whispered.

"Is she still sleeping?" Dustin asked excitement in his voice.

"You can go check, but don't wake her," admonished Lacey.

Dixie stepped back in her room, slipped out of her robe, and back under the covers. Dustin stealthily entered her room and walked around her bed peering at her to see is she was still asleep. Reassured he left quickly to give his report. Dixie lie still beneath the covers wondering how long she would have to wait for her breakfast to appear.

Moments later the door opened.

"Mom, wake up," Dustin shouted. "We brung you breakfast."

"Brought," Dixie corrected smiling as she sat up.

Lacey placed the tray across Dixie's lap saying, "Ta-da breakfast is served."

"Why thank you both very much," Dixie's smile widened as she looked at the breakfast before her. Scrambled eggs, toast with jam, and apple sauce.

Ellen Jean entered with as steaming cup of coffee to complete the meal. “You two head to the kitchen so your food doesn’t get cold,” she said playfully. When Lacey and Dustin scampered out of the room, she looked a Dixie and asked, “Where’s the car?”

“Darn,” Dixie muttered, “someone slit the tires last night. We’re going to have to walk to church.”

“No problem. The kids will think it’s an adventure.”

Dixie smiled her appreciation. Ellen Jean left to join the kids in the kitchen. She ate quickly and dressed for church. Then, she went to help get Lacey and Dustin ready.

They stepped out of the house and onto the porch, when a black car pulled into the driveway. Tom got out saying, “Morning, everyone, I thought you might be needing a lift to church.”

The kids were running toward the car. Tom opened the back door. Dixie hesitated a moment, then smiled and said, “Thank you kindly, Tom.”

Tom shut the back door and went around to open the door for Dixie. She thought he looked nice in his blue suit, his grey hair neatly in place. Much different from the t-shirt and jeans he usually wore.

Arriving at church Tom let them out in front, then parked the car. Dixie and the children went inside. Ellen Jean joined her friends. Lacey and Dustin got in line with Dixie to be seated.

Dixie looked for Tom, but he was nowhere around. Although she disliked turning in the pew to watch people coming in, she did so today, looking for Tom. He did not falter a step as he came down the aisle to join her and the kids. Here in the Junction, Tom was making a *big* statement. Joining her in church as much as said, *"I'm looking out for Dixie."*

After the service was over, they mingled with friends and neighbors waiting for Ellen Jean, Lacey, and Dustin to join them. Once they were altogether, Tom went to get the car.

Ellen Jean spoke first, "Will Tom be staying for dinner?"

"Will he, Mom?" Dustin chimed in.

Just then, Tom pulled up, got out and opened the back door for the children. Then, he went to open the door for Dixie. Once everyone was in the car, Tom drove away.

"Tom, will you join us for Sunday dinner?" Dixie asked.

He paused, then asked, "How do the children feel about it?"

Dustin piped up, "We'd like it a lot."

The girls echoed Dustin with their approval.

Tom looked at Dixie, " Then, I'd be delighted. I should tell you I sent my cook over with some things, so dinner should be about ready when we get there. I had your brother let her in. Hope you don't mind."

Dixie was taken aback at the presumption he could just take over, but the thought of someone else making Sunday dinner felt like a blessing so she withheld the reprimand. "That was thoughtful of you, Tom," she said honestly.

The rest of the drive was silent. At home the children changed out of their church clothes, then ran to the backyard to play. Ellen Jean came with a request to invite Billy Owens for dinner. Dixie told her yes, if she set the table and checked in the kitchen to see if help was needed.

Dixie went to the kitchen for a tray of lemonade and two glasses, "Tom will you join me on the front porch?" she asked.

Tom opened the door for her. Once outside her took the tray from her and set it on a small table. He let her do the honors of pouring. After Dixie sat down, she felt suddenly nervous. Finally, she said, "It was a fine thing you did in church for us today. Thank you."

"It weren't nothin' but it will keep the biddies tongues waggin' for a while." He tipped his glass smiled and took a drink.

"No one has stood up for us before, not since my parents died."

"The were fine people who would be proud of what you and Junior have accomplished," Tom replied.

"They would be proud of Junior. He made a go of the farm, got married, they have one son and a baby on the way. He even finished his Associates Degree," Dixie said her voice filled with pride.

"Dixie, you had no way of knowin' your man was a con. He had us all fooled. Then you showed up with a black eye and some silly excuse about tripp' on a toy. We knew then, he should be gone. You have nothin' to be ashamed for."

"I'm stuck with him. He gets out of jail in another five years," Dixie said pensively. "The little ones hardly remember him now."

"Divorce him, Dixie," Tom said bluntly.

"It takes money, Tom. I don't have enough," she shrugged helplessly. *Money she'd never have enough.*

Tom sipped his lemonade until Mrs. Kemp, his cook, came out to tell them dinner was ready. They walked toward the dining room, both smiling when they heard Mrs. Kemp, "You children skedaddle into the bathroom and wash up before you eat."

Billy arrived just as they were sitting down and held Ellen Jean's chair for her. Lacey stood by her chair hoping her brother would get the hint. It was Tom who stepped forward to assist her. Lacey hissed at Dustin, "You should be doing this."

Dustin grinned and pulled a roll onto his plate. Lacey fumed but said nothing else.

Mrs. Kemp cleared up after dinner. Ellen Jean and Billy went for a walk. Lacey and Dustin returned to play in the backyard. Dixie and Tom had coffee at the now empty table.

"As soon as Mrs. Kemp is done, she's going to drive me home," Tom said quietly.

"Why would she do that when your car is here?" Dixie asked surprised.

Tom pushed his keys across the table to her. "You need a way to get around until your car is fixed. I got my truck at home."

Tears welled in Dixie's eyes as she started to protest, "Tom, I couldn't..."

"Haven' me look out for you means I aim to help," he stated firmly. "It's past time someone did."

"Thank you," she said smiling through her tears. She stood, walked to Tom, and gave him a hug, " You're a good man, Tom Brennan."

Tom blushed as he hugged her back. Moments later, he left with Mrs. Kemp.

When Ellen Jean returned and Billy had gone home, she helped Dixie make lunches for school.

"So, how does this thing with you and Tom work?" she asked curiously.

Dixie glanced up from the sandwich she was making, "What thing?"

"You know, him watching out for you."

"Tom Brennan is a good man with a big heart. He's just helping out until the car can be fixed," Dixie answered.

"Oh, Dixie, get real. Tom is sweet on you. What's he going to want in return?" asked Ellen Jean.

Dixie stopped what she was doing and stared at her sister. "Tom is not sweet on my. He's just being a friend."

"If you say so."

"I do. Now off with you," Dixie told her. *Where did Ellen Jean get the idea Tom was more than a friend?*

Dixie was twenty-nine. Her husband, Robert Hawkins, had been in jail since Lacey was three and Dustin not a year old. He still had another five years before he would be eligible for parole. He wasted his life. *Was she wasting hers, too?*

Chapter 3

The phone rang after the kids got off to school. Dixie picked up the receiver in the living room. "Hello?"

"Dixie Hawkins, please," said a male voice.

"This is Dixie."

"I'm a friend of Robert's. I was hoping to stop in and see you."

"I'd rather you didn't," was Dixie's firm reply.

"That's not very neighborly. Robert said you'd be able to help me out," the man continued.

"Robert doesn't live here. Good-bye," Dixie hung up the phone. Angrily she marched down the hallway to get the laundry basket.

The phone was ringing when she returned. Still angry she paused before picking it up. "Hello," she rasped sharply.

"Good morning, Dixie. This is Edie at Ned Parson's office," came the chipper reply.

"Hi, Edie, how are you?" Dixie responded warmly.

"I'm fine. Ned wants to know if he could stop by sometime today," Edie responded.

"Sure, I guess," Dixie hesitated. "Do you know what he wants?"

"Nope, he just asked to see if you'd be home," she answered.

"I'll be here. Dustin gets home from kindergarten about twelve-thirty," she offered.

"Okay, I'll tell Ned to be there at eleven, then he'll be gone before Dustin get home," Ellen said.

"Eleven is good," Dixie agreed. She hung up the phone wondering what Ned wanted and set off to start the laundry. She'd know soon enough.

Ned Parsons was a portly man in his mid-fifties. He arrived promptly at eleven. Dixie ushered him into her living room and asked, "Can I get you some coffee, Mr. Parsons?"

"Coffee would be nice, but can we sit at your table?" he asked.

"Sure," Dixie agreed leading the way to the kitchen. She got cups and poured coffee as Ned settled himself at the table and opened his briefcase.

After she poured coffee and settled at the table, Ned began, "Dixie, you need to think about the future."

Surprised, Dixie replied, "I do it every day."

"Don't you think it's time you divorced Robert and moved on."

Dixie was speechless. *Who did this man think he was?*

"I'm sorry to be blunt," Ned continued unaware of her reaction. "Robert is a convicted criminal and it won't do having him around you and the children."

Of all the pompous statements, Dixie felt her anger rising. "Mr. Parsons, let me get this straight," Dixie started *she was sure steam was coming out her ears.* "You are here asking ne to get a divorce?"

"Why, yes! Isn't that what you want?" he asked looking at her red face.

"What I want isn't the issue, I don't have the finances for a divorce or I would have done it when Rob was convicted," she exploded.

“Money is not a problem,” he reassured her reaching out to pat her hand.

“It might not be a problem for you; however *I* am responsible for three children,” she answered hotly.

“No, what I mean is, I’ll help you at no charge,” he told her a bit flustered by her reaction.

“Why?” Dixie asked suspiciously.

“Because it’s the right thing to do,” he responded.

“The right thing for whom?” she demanded.

“For you and the children,” was his smug reply.

Dixie was still angry and wondered, *Did Tom send Ned Parsons to her door? If so, did he pay the man, too?* When she finally spoke again, she asked, “Did Tom Brennan send you? Did he pay you to come?”

Ned looked startled, “No, I haven’t talked to Tom. What makes you ask?”

“Frankly, you’ve never offered to help before.”

Looking flustered, he shuffled some papers, then said, “Maybe I shouldn’t have come.”

Dixie’s anger had ebbed. “No, you just caught me off guard. I never thought I would be free of Rob.”

“You can and I’ll help,” he offered enthusiastically.

“Tell me what I need to do,” Dixie said before he had a chance to change his mind.

Ned Parsons had repacked his briefcase and was on his way out the door as Dustin’s bus dropped him off. He came running up the driveway yelling, “Hey, Mom, guess what!” He stopped when he saw Mr. Parsons.

"I'll call you in a couple of days, Dixie," he said over his shoulder as he walked toward his car. *Now,* he thought, *my wife will stop nagging me.*

Dixie looked at Dustin, "So, what's the big news?"

"We're going to a farm next week," he said excitedly.

"You've been to Uncle John's farm," she reminded him.

"I know, Mom, that's why it's so cool," his eyes sparkled as he replied.

"What's so cool?" she asked. Getting information from Dustin always took time.

"We're going to Uncle John's farm and I get to be the 'sistant guide," he blurted barely containing his excitement.

Dixie smiled, "Wow, that is a big deal! How about some lunch? Then you can help me make a special dinner to celebrate."

Dustin was in the house like a flash. He started setting silverware on the table. As they sat down to soup with peanut butter and jam sandwiches, Dustin asked, "Who was that man?"

"Mr. Parsons is a lawyer who is helping me with some business," she answered.

"Well, I like Mr. Tom better," declared Dustin.

She ruffled his hair answering, "So do I, Buddy."

Chapter 4

Dixie finished the laundry and put the dinner on, so they could eat as soon as the girls got home. Dustin was playing in his room, when Dixie was interrupted from putting the clothes away by a knock on the door.

She walked across the room to open the door only to find a stranger standing there. “Can I help you?” she asked.

“Hawk didn’t tell me you were beautiful,” he said turning on the charm.

“Excuse me?” Dixie was instantly suspicious.

“I’m sorry. Name’s Mace. I’m a friend of Rob’s,” he said smoothly.

“Did you call me this morning?” she asked.

“I did. I was sure if we met, you’d help me,” he said arrogantly.

Dixie looked him up and down. About five foot ten she thought. Dark, swarthy type thinks he can charm me. She eased onto the porch closing the door behind her.

“You were wrong,” she stated firmly. “I want nothing to do with Rob or his friends. Please leave.”

The bus carrying Ellen Jean arrived at just then. Billy Owens got off the bus with her.

“Hey, Dixie!” Billy yelled.

Mace was momentarily distracted. Ellen Jean and Billy quickly came up the driveway.

“Who’s your friend?” Billy asked eyeing the stranger.

“Someone who was just leaving,” Dixie replied, “and won’t be returning.”

Mace shrugged. “See you around, Dixie. He walked to a beat up brown truck, got in, and drove off.

Dixie couldn’t read the license plate for the dirt, but knew it was a Ford.

“Who was that?” Ellen Jean asked, concern in her voice.

“Some friend of Rob’s who called this morning and asked to come by. I told him no. He didn’t listen,” she answered watching the truck disappear.

Billy spoke up, “You need to contact the police.”

“And tell them what? Someone claiming to know my husband stopped by.”

“I see your point,” he said discouraged.

“Let’s see about dinner. Billy, are you staying?” Dixie asked.

“Yeah, let me call my ma,” he said pulling out his cell phone.

Dixie went inside wondering, *What’s next?*

When Billy disconnected, Ellen Jean asked, “Can you call Tom Brennan and tell him?”

“Sure.” He punched the number for information. Ellen Jean went to help Dixie as Billy made the call. He came in with Lacey who had just arrived on her bus. Nothing more was said about the incident.

Chapter 5

Dixie was surprised to see Mike behind the bar when she came in. She waved on her way to punch in. Mike nodded and continued pouring drinks.

"Where's Tom?" Dixie asked when she stepped to the bar with her first order of the night.

"Had some business, be in later," Mike answered as he filled her order.

Dixie kept busy. She was pleased to see Hank and his buddies were not in tonight. It was early so she had a few orders for burgers, fish, shrimp, and fries, so she was between the kitchen and the bar.

Donna worked half the room. There was not much time for chat. The lull came about eight. By then Tom was behind the bar and Dixie was busy bussing a couple of empty tables.

"Get your car fixed?" Donna asked.

"It's at Joe's," Dixie replied.

"Hear Tom made his intentions known in church," said Donna curious about gossip.

"He took us and sat with us if that's what you're asking."

"I knew it!" Donna exclaimed. "He's been sweet on you for a while."

Dixie said nothing and continued working. Then she took a short break to call home. After saying goodnight to each of the kids, she asked Ellen Jean, "Any visitors?"

"Nope," she replied. "We're fine, Dixie."

Feeling somewhat relieved Dixie headed back into the bar. There on a stool flirting with Donna sat Mace.

She went back to work. Tom noticed Dixie avoided the area near the new guy.

"Dix, everything okay?" Tom asked.

She glanced at Tom, smiled, and said, "Right as rain." Picked up her drinks and headed to deliver them.

Mace waved for another beer. When Tom brought it, he asked, "Known Dixie long?"

"Lived here all my life. Know most everyone," Tom answered.

"Rob never told me how pretty she is," Mace said watching Dixie.

Tom snorted, "Him. Fool didn't know what he had."

Mace picked up the scorn in Tom's voice, "I sure wouldn't have let her go."

Looking at the man suspiciously, Tom made a round of drinks for Donna.

"She been the faithful wife?" Mace asked his tone implying differently.

"How's it your business?" Tom asked moving off but keeping his eye on the guy.

The evening went without a hitch until they headed for the parking lot. Mace was leaning against Tom's car. Dixie turned to Tom and whispered, "Will you follow me home?"

"Sure thing," he answered heading for his truck.

"Dixie, I was hoping you'd invite me home," Mace said seductively.

"I thought I made it clear, I don't want you around," she shot back as she got into the car.

"Don't be that way, Dixie, I know you're lonely," he continued.

"Ha! You know nothing," she said getting in the car and slamming the door.

Tom pulled up and honked. Mace stepped back as Dixie put the car in reverse and drove out of the parking lot. Tom following in his truck.

So, Dixie had a protector. Mace would get rid of him quick enough. All he needed was some time alone at Dixie's and he would have the hidden bank stash. He might even have a bit of fun with Dixie before he split.

Chapter 6

Dixie waited on the sidewalk for Tom. “Thanks. You want some coffee?”

“Don’t need coffee, but would like to talk,” he told her.

Once inside, Dixie went down the hall to check on the kids and Ellen Jean. They were sleeping soundly. She went into the den and found Billy fast asleep on the pullout sofa.

She headed to the kitchen where she found Tom seated at the table. “Sure you don’t want something? I’ve got sweet tea and lemonade,” she offered again.

“Glass of sweet tea’ll be fine,” he answered.

Dixie brought two glasses to the table. Tom took one as she sat down.

“Who’s the fella?” Tom asked.

“Some no account friend of Rob’s who thinks I have something of value,” Dixie answered. “His name is Mace. He called this morning and I told him to get lost. He showed up this afternoon but took off when Ellen Jean and Billy showed up.”

“He’s going to be trouble,” said Tom.

“Probably,” she agreed.

“Notify the police before this gets out of hand.”

“Could he have slit my tires?” Dixie asked.

“Might have,” Tom replied. “Call the police when I leave. Tell ‘em you got a prowler and describe this Mace fella. Tell ‘em he’s been harassing you by phone, showed up at the house, and later at work. They’ll send someone to check and you tell ‘em to keep watch for a few days.” He stood to leave.

Dixie stood, too saying, “Thanks, Tom. I hate to keep dragging you into my troubles.”

“My pleasure,” he said smiling.

She walked him to the door and turned out the porch light when he was gone. Hesitating for a minute before calling the police. They sent someone to get specifics. After an hour, the police had gone. Dixie fell into bed and a fitful sleep.

Chapter 7

It was almost time for Dustin's bus when the phone rang. "Hello?" Dixie said.

"Dixie, it wasn't nice to send the cops after me," Mace hissed. "Now we are going to play this my way."

She hung up the phone. The bus driver tooted the horn and Dixie went to the door to greet Dustin. The phone was ringing when they got inside.

"I'll get it!" Dustin said running for the phone.

"No!" Dixie shouted.

Dustin stopped to look at his mom. As he did, the phone stopped ringing and a man came in the front door. Dustin didn't know what to say.

The man said, "You should have let him answer it, Dixie."

Turning Dixie said, "Get out of my house."

"Is this the way to treat a friend?" Mace continued.

"You're not a friend. You're trespassing." She took a step toward him once more saying, "Get out!"

"We got some unfinished business," he said closing the front door.

Without blinking Dixie said, "Dustin, tool shed."

He was gone out the back door in a flash.

"Cute, the way he took off. Is there where you're keeping the money?"

"What money?"

"Don't play coy with me. Rob told me you're holding his share of the take from the bank until he gets home."

Dixie started laughing hysterically. She took a seat on the arm of the chair to keep her balance.

"I don't see anything funny," Mace said menacingly.

"There no money," she managed to say.

"You're not a good liar, Dixie," he said stepping forward and grabbing her arm. "How long before the kid comes back?"

"He's not coming back," she answered trying to jerk her arm free.

"Yeah and I believe that," Mace sneered. "Well, if he comes back too soon, he's going to learn about the birds and the bees." He grasped her arm tighter and started to drag her down the hallway.

Dixie grabbed every door jamb putting up a good fight. As he shoved her into her room, she went limp. He caught her in his arms, and Dixie acted quickly kneeing him in the crotch. As he doubled over, she grabbed the brass lamp from her dresser and bashed him in the head. She had him hog-tied in minutes and stood over him as she called the police. Mace cursed her between moans.

Mace was arrested for breaking and entering as well as attempted assault.

What the Storm Blew In

To Mike McCormack

I’ve waited a lifetime…

Chapter 1

Lily Collins sat on the window seat looking out at the ocean. It had been a stormy night two years ago when a man had dragged himself onto the shore as the tide came in. She sounded the alarm, grabbing blankets, and a first aid kit as she rushed out the door. Her long blonde hair blowing in her face as she to the beach with medical supplies and other things she knew she would need to save him.

As she reached the man, he rolled and looked into her eyes. "Are you an angel?" he gasped and lost consciousness.

Looking up, Lily saw her father and several men approaching her. Her father, Gordon Collins, carried a litter as he raced through the wind and rain to reach her. Lily busily began to check the man's arms and legs for broken bones. She sighed finding none. Then tried listening to his breathing, it was shallow, but his pulse was steady.

"Can we move him?" her father shouted to be heard above the wind.

"He doesn't seem to have any broken bones, but I believe he is dehydrated," she screamed trying to be heard.

The men quickly lifted the stranger into the litter. Lily packed blankets around him and they headed back. The storm was getting worse and each of them held onto the litter to keep from being blown away with the winds. It had been a while since they had a nor'easter. This was going to be a bad one.

Chapter 2

Collins Pointe was a small island off the coast of Maine. Why anyone ever tried to settle the rock was a guess. People bicycled around the island or walked. Most people could trace their ancestors back probably to the first deep sea fishermen. It is believed Jonas Collins, Lily's great-great-great grandfather found the island during a storm and saved his crew by making it to the cove. Later the crew followed Collins as he chose to bring his family to the island and make it his home. Fishing boats still left each morning and returned at night. Being somewhat in from the ocean itself, the island was protected from most winter storms. Few boats or ships found their way into the harbor.

While the storm whipped outside, the men carried the stranger into Gordon Collins' home and put him in the guest room. Lily put water on to boil while the men stripped the stranger and put him between the sheets.

"He's pretty tore up from the rocks," she heard one of the men say.

"Looks like he's tough," another commented.

"Does he have any identification?" Gordon Collins asked.

"If he did, he lost it in the water," the first man replied.

Lily entered the room carrying two hot water bottles, she lifted the sheet at the foot of the bed and placed one there, the other she placed near the man's thigh. "Scoot," she ordered using her hands to push the men from the room. "Bring me dry blankets."

Muttering the men left the room, her father returned a moment later with a blanket and an old quilt her grandmother made.

She took them saying, “Thanks, Dad.”

He turned knowing the man would be safe under Lily’s ministrations. Gordon Collins spared nothing in getting his daughter the best education money could buy. She was the only doctor on the island, and he was proud of her.

Heading to his office, Gordon, notified the Coast Guard of a man washed ashore and if they knew of any boats in the area that might have capsized. Not getting the answer he was hoping for, he went to the kitchen to make coffee. Once Lily had her patient settled, she would sit all night with him. His job would be to keep the coffee coming and relieve her for brief naps.

Chapter 3

When the young man awoke early the next morning, the first person he saw was Lily. “You’re the angel I saw,” he croaked.

Quickly Lily lifted a glass of water and tilted his head so he could drink. Saying, “I’m Lily Collins the doctor here on Collins Pointe.”

She eased him back onto the pillow. Reaching around her neck for her stethoscope she took his arm to determine his blood pressure. Taking the stethoscope out of her ears she said, “Well, you have a strong heartbeat.” Then reached to take his pulse. Finding them both in order she rose.

He grabbed her arm, “Please, don’t go.”

“I’m just going to put on some broth, so we can start building your strength up,” she told him, gently removing in his hand from her arm. “I won’t be gone long.”

Gordon entered as Lily left. “I see you made it. Can you tell me your name?”

“Luke Cavendish,” he replied. “How did I get here? The last thing I remember is toasting my friend, Adam Holcomb’s upcoming wedding.”

“Where and when were you doing this toasting,” Gordon inquired.

“On Adam’s yacht, just outside Portland.”

“Were you cruising or in port?” Gordon kept the questions coming.

“The plan was to cruise the harbor, then meet his fiancée and my date for a late dinner. I don’t know what happened.” Luke sat up then grabbed his head.

"Lie, down, Son," Gordon said putting a gentle hand on his shoulder. "I suspect you have a nasty concussion. I'll do some checking. Do you know the name of the yacht?"

Luke rested his head on the pillow, "Annabelle, after his mother."

"Lily will be back shortly. Listen to her, she's a good doctor."

Lying on the bed, Luke closed his eyes. *What happened? He remembered getting up to give the toast.* It was his first drink of the evening. *Adam, Justin, and Wesley were all there. Justin was at the helm. Did he shout? Was something wrong? Why couldn't he remember?*

Chapter 4

While Luke mulled how he ended up in the icy waters of the Atlantic, Gordon radioed the Coast Guard to let them know the name of their water-logged friend.

Lily came in as her father ended the radio transmission. “What did you learn?”

“It’s not good,” he said worry causing him to frown. “Luke was on board the Annabelle with his friends. Evidently, they were boarded after radioing for assistance. It’s shaky as to what happened next, but there was an explosion. One of his friends is dead, another is paralyzed from the waist down, as third one lost a leg, and Luke has been reported missing and presumed dead. He is one hundred fifty miles from the accident.”

“Oh, goodness,” Lily’s hand went to her mouth. “He doesn’t remember, does he?”

“Not much at this point,” her father confirmed. “Worst news is Luke is the son of James Stuart Cavendish who will arriving via helicopter as soon as weather permits.”

Lily’s face showed disgust. The Cavendish family wanted to ban fishing off the coast of Portland. They wanted to take the livelihood of men like her father who eked out a living by catching fish. Men who battled storm and sea to bring home a big enough catch to keep them in food throughout the winter. Even with the mail junket coming all summer to bring stores of food and medicine, they were hard pressed to make it through some winters. A Cavendish washing up on the shore was bad news, a second one coming to invade their island was going to be worse. Lily left the room to check on her patient. She knew the worst for him was not over yet.

Luke was asleep when Lily entered the room. She reached out to touch his forehead only to discover he was burning with fever. Something she expected once he was warm. Gently she put a cold compress to his forehead. She would do her best to help his body fight the fever before giving him medicine. It was going to be a long day.

Chapter 5

Two years had passed since Luke Cavendish washed up on the shore of Collins Pointe. Lily found herself in awe of the things which happened since then. Luke's father arrived full of steam and attempted to bully his way around. What Lily found was a man who cared deeply for his only son. He had medical supplies brought out and conferred with Gordon and the other islanders to find the best location for a medical facility. Then he built one.

It was state of the art and his way of showing his gratitude. He set up a fund of some sort to make sure the needed supplies were always on hand. With his help the community was able to store more food supplies. The mail junket which in the past came weekly, now ran Monday, Wednesday, and Friday.

Seeing the need for a place to stay, James Cavendish bought a piece of land and built a rooming house. Then brought in people to train some of the islanders how to run it. Finally, he deeded the house back to the people of the island. Her opinion of him changed deeply.

Lily was amazed this man would become her father-in-law in a few hours. Luke fully recovered, returned to the mainland and the life he knew. However, it was just a short month when he stepped off the junket and booked a room at the boarding house. He wanted to learn how to live what he termed it a normal life. With him, he brought knowledge and money to make Collins Pointe a thriving seaport. He also set out to woo the beautiful doctor who had saved his life.

It had been difficult as Lily was not looking for a suitor. She loved the island and its people. It was her home. She spent seven years on the mainland attending first college then medical school. She was not unaware of the world outside her tiny town. She had interned at Boston Medical. The fast pace of the city and bright commercialism did not make her want to stay. Lily believed Luke's fascination with her was just a whim. He was used to an upper-class life. He was part of the elite. Lily was just different from the women he was used to being around.

She spent her spare time learning about the herbs on the island and which ones she could use for medicinal purposes. She learned how to process and a cultivate them. It seemed she was being shadowed each time she was away from the clinic. Luke wanted to know all there was about Lily. He started asking teachers about her. Then he asked people on the island. If they thought it strange, they said nothing. He had recently taken to following her when she went scouting for herbs. Finally, Lily decided to stop it. She sent an invitation to the boarding house inviting Luke to come for lunch.

He arrived on time looking comfortable in jeans and flannel shirt. His dark hair wavy and his brown eyes intense. He handed her a bouquet of yellow roses having learned they were her favorite.

Lily led him to the dining room overlooking the shoreline. "Please have a seat. Would you like a cup of coffee?" She hoped she didn't sound as nervous as she felt.

"I'll have whatever you're having," he told her smiling.

She forgot the devastation his smile could cause. Reaching for two cups she handed him one. “Help yourself while I put the roses in a vase.”

He took a seat at the dining room table and watched as she put the roses in water, then poured coffee and put in on a tray with cream and sugar to bring to the table.

“I wasn’t sure if you liked cream and sugar with your coffee,” she told him while setting the tray on the table.

“Of course, you didn’t,” he answered with a grin. “Can I help you with something?”

She was flustered by his smile. “I have it under control. Thanks.” She walked to the kitchen where she had chicken salad sandwiches prepared and a spinach salad to go with it. She put them on the tray and carried them to the dining room. She put Luke’s in front of him and hers on the opposite side, then put the tray on the counter before sitting down.

He surprised her by asking if she wanted him to say grace.

“By all means,” she said bowing her head.

“Dear Heavenly Father, thank you for the food we are to partake, let it nourish our bodies. May you help Lily see I mean her no harm. I just want to get to know her. Amen.”

Lily blushed. Then took a drink of her coffee. Taking a deep breath, she said, “Mr. Cavendish, I don’t know why you are bothering the town trying to find out about me. I am no one of importance, just a simple country doctor. I use modern medicine and herbs to treat my patients.”

“There is no need to call me, Mr. Cavendish, surely you can call me Luke,” he replied. “As to you being a simple country doctor, nothing could be further from the truth. I have it on good authority you are a hard worker, a dedicated doctor, and the most beautiful woman on the island."

"Your flattery with get you nowhere," she assured him. Reaching for her sandwich to take a bite, she watched him for a reaction.

He was halfway through a bite in his sandwich and unable to reply. Lily smiled and bit into hers.

When Luke swallowed, he looked at Lily knowing she waited for him to comment, "I don't give away flattery, Lily. I only tell you what I learned from your friends and neighbors."

"Just about anyone who will talk to you," she snapped. "I don't like you prying into my private life. I've seen how rich playboys of your ilk behave. It's a lifestyle better suited to Boston or New York. It's not going to work with me."

Luke put down his sandwich, drank from his cup of coffee, and spoke softly, "Is that what you really think of me? I'm a rich playboy out to score with the beautiful doctor so I can add it to my trophy wall. You haven't taken time to find out anything about me. Yes, I was born to wealthy parents, however I earned my way through college with my brain on scholarship. I went to work in the "real" world and built my company from the ground up. I'm not looking to score with you or any other woman. I don't need trophies." He stood up and walked out of the house leaving Lily to stare after him.

Stunned Lily didn't move for a few minutes. *Had she really passed judgement on someone without giving them the benefit of doubt? What was it about this man which set her off? How did he manage to keep her off balance all the time?*

She finished her lunch and did the dishes. Still wondering what had just a happened in her dining room. She had things to do which did not allow dwelling on Luke Cavendish. She changed clothes and went to her lab at the medical center. She also knew she had patients to see.

As she checked lab results and x-rays, Lily kept hearing snippets of conversation. "Have you seen that nice Mr. Cavendish today? The young man smitten with Dr. Collins?"

"Mr. Cavendish was in earlier making sure all our supplies were arriving on time." This was followed by a nervous giggle.

Honestly, Lily thought, *you would think Luke Cavendish was some kind of God.* She stopped herself short. *What did she really know about Luke Cavendish? He'd been tossed on the beach after a nor'easter. While recovering his father had shown up and managed to update many things on the island making life better for everyone. Luke was handsome and charming. He'd gone out of his way to learn about things which were special or important to me. He'd even move his business (whatever it is) to the island. Why did Lily find herself so put off by him? Or was it merely interest?* Shaking her head to clear her thoughts, Lily continued to see the two patients they had. Mary Lou Watkins and her new son, Mason. Both were doing well and would be discharged in the morning.

When did the island start revolving around Luke Cavendish? Lily puzzled over this as she walked home. She was not one who usually judged people without a cause, but when Mr. Cavendish sailed into port and spent millions making it what he deemed fit to live, Lily's hackles came up. She painted the son in the figure of his father, meaning money and creature comforts meant more to him than people. Lily was going to owe Luke an apology but was going to need a better approach. Inviting him to lunch again was out of the question, she'd have to come up with something else.

Chapter 6

Luke was stunned by Lily's words. He never his wanting to know about her put him in a playboy category. He abhorred men his age who did the things Lily accused him of doing. *The nerve of the woman. Who does she think she is? Queen of the island? He'd stay out of her direct path for a while, but he was going to give her every reason to regret her words.* Luke had his business to tend to, but he could be around to check on things. People on the island would mention him in passing especially if he dropped in at the medical center. When he left Lily's, he found his way to the medical center cafeteria. Several employees knew him, so he didn't lack for company. He joined them and they shared jokes and tales with him. He could enjoy his food and not endure insults.

Lily spent the next few days hearing the wonders of Luke Cavendish from everyone she met. She decided to take the Wednesday junket to the mainland. She needed a break from Luke and wanted to find out more about him. She would be gone until Friday which would give her time to do some sleuthing of her own. Two could play at this game. It might put a damper on some of the guilt she felt at the possibility she misjudged him.

Her first stop was to see Luke's father. The quarterly report on the medical clinic was due. While she usually mailed it, this time she chose to deliver it in person. She called ahead from the dock to make sure she could see him. Now arriving at his impressive office, Lily wondered if she had made a mistake in coming here. Taking a deep breath, she entered the lion's den.

She gave the receptionist her name and the next thing she knew James Cavendish was stepping out of the elevator to greet her.

"Lily, this is a wonderful surprise," he said hugging her. "I hope nothing is wrong."

"Not a thing," she responded with a smile when he let her go. "I came to deliver the quarterly report and spend some time on the mainland."

"Come on up, we'll dispense with the report," he said ushering her into the elevator. Once inside he asked, "Is there something else you need?

"I'm on a fishing trip," she responded. "I want to learn more about your son."

"Ah," James said. "I gather he's been asking about you?"

"How did you know?"

"Come to my office, we'll take care of business then go to lunch," he said as the doors opened. Inside the office James motioned Lily to a chair near his desk, then took one next to her. "There was no reason for you to deliver this report in person was there?"

Lily blushed, "None at all."

"Good. I'll give it to my secretary have her call in a reservation for lunch and the car service." He took the file Lily had been holding and walked to the door. There he asked his secretary to take care of the report, call for lunch reservations for two, and call the car service. He turned to Lily asking, "Will you join me?" They took the elevator to the garage level where the car was waiting for them. The driver opened the door for them to get in, closed the door, and returned to the driver's seat.

Once seated he asked, “Straight to the restaurant, Sir?”

“No, drive through the historic home district.”

“As you wish,” he started the car.

“Lily, I want you to see the restored homes we have here. I think they are exquisite,” James told her.

“I’d like to see them,” Lily said wondering which of the exquisite homes would belong to the Cavendish family. She expected it would be lavish since they had the money. The neighborhood was everything James said it would be. The homes were restored to their glory and the lawns were immaculate.

They arrived at the restaurant where the driver let them out and the maître de led them to their table. The waiter brought a wine list and told them the specials. Once they ordered, James began, “Luke is not like most rich men. He would not take my money for college. He earned scholarships and worked part-time to pay for his education. It was as if he wanted to prove he could do it on his own. While his buddies were living large, Luke was working and studying.”

“I’m glad to hear he had initiative,” Lily commented reaching for her wine glass. “I was afraid he was one of those spoiled rich kids, who think they rule everyone they come in contact with.”

“Nothing of the sort,” James assured her. “After lunch, I’ll have the driver take us back by my home on the way to the office.”

“You don’t live in the historic district?”

“I could but I choose a different lifestyle from the people who live there,” James told her.

Lunch was served and they were quiet. On the drive back to the office, Lily was amazed at the neighborhood Luke grew up in. It was an average middle-class neighborhood with some houses maintained better than others. All of them looked warm and inviting. It was much different than the lifestyle she had envisioned for him. Again, she found herself questioning her own judgement.

As they pulled up in front of the office, James asked, "Is there someplace my driver can drop you off?"

"I'm just returning to my hotel. Friday, I take the junket back to the island," answered Lily.

"Fine, just tell him the name of your hotel. I enjoyed out lunch," James said. He stepped from the car and walked into his building.

"Where to, Miss?" the driver asked.

She told him the name of the hotel and leaned into the seat to ponder her troubled thoughts. There was more to Luke Cavendish than met the eye.

Chapter 7

The next six months became a game of cat and mouse between Lilly and Luke. She was sure to be where he was going to be. Often, she would be with another gentleman, whom she would introduce to Luke. It didn't take Luke long to figure out what Lily was up to, so he arranged to be where she was in the company of a lady friend. He did not limit his friends to any age category.

Finally, Luke had enough. He arranged for a female friend of his and Lily's to invite her to a picnic lunch in the park. Time and date were included on the note. Luke had her favorite sandwiches made from the deli, picked her favorite dessert from the bakery, a bottle of her favorite wine, cheese and crackers, and set off for the park an hour early. He spread a blanket on the ground and set up two plates, putting the wine in a pail of ice to keep it chilled. Then he walked away to set up a camera on a timer. He wanted photos of the two of them enjoying a picnic lunch. Surveying everything, he knew it was perfect. All he had to do was wait for Lily to arrive. Luke turned to look out at the sea which had blown him onto shore.

Lily took a step into the area and saw Luke standing there. She gasped saying, "I'm sorry I must have mistaken the directions."

"No mistake, Lily," he answered without turning around.

"You sent the note?"

"Yes. I was hoping we could talk." He turned to look at her.

Lily blushed, "We probably should."

He took two steps toward her and motioned her to sit. Then he turned to the task of opening the wine and starting the camera. When he was done, he handed her a glass. Tipping his own toward it saying, “To new beginnings.”

Clinking their glasses, Lily whispered, “To new beginnings.”

Luke turned to the task of taking out the cheese, crackers, sandwiches, and salad, and spreading it on the blanket. He handed Lily silverware and a napkin.

“What were you thinking about when I walked up?” she asked putting some cheese on a cracker.

“How lucky I was to have made it ashore and how God was watching over me the night you found me.”

“It was pretty fortunate I was looking out the window.”

He smiled, “I think I’d have died on the beach had you not been.”

“Exposure would have played a big part in whether you survived,” Lily agreed. “By the time you hit the shore you’d been exposed more than your fair share already.”

“I still don’t remember it,” Luke confessed. “Just looking up and seeing you.”

“All I know is what the Coast Guard was able to tell us. You and your friends were boarded in the harbor and taken out to sea. You were the lucky one,” she told him.

“Lucky to be alive, yes. But to have lost part of my life, not so.”

“Somethings might better be forgotten.”

“You are right, so can we forget about the lunch at your house?” He winked at her as he said it.

"Absolutely!"

"Good. I understand you had lunch with my father a few months back."

"He was kind enough to offer it when I delivered the quarterly reports."

"I'm glad you are getting to know him," Luke said. "He thinks the world of you."

"Only because I was here when his only son needed a doctor," she assured him reaching for a sandwich. "Mmmmm," she said biting into it.

They talked as they ate, and Lily helped Luke pick up when they were done. He took her hand and they walked along the beach. When they returned to the picnic area, Luke said, "I have truly enjoyed this, Lily."

She turned to him smiling, "As have I."

He leaned into kiss her and Lily found herself anticipating the kiss. Luke kept it a short kiss and Lily was disappointed.

They held hands as Luke walked Lily back to the medical center. Then he returned to get his camera and take care of the picnic supplies. His next stop was getting the photos developed at a one-hour shop. They were all he hoped and had double prints with one copy for Lily.

Lily made her rounds and walked home. She found she was too distracted after her lunch with Luke. She wished it could have gone longer. In spite of herself, she found his company pleasant. Hopefully they could see each other again.

Chapter 8

The next morning Lily found the clinic a buzz. As she made her way to her office, she felt the eyes of every staff member on her. She wondered what on earth she had done. Opening her office door, she was stunned. The room was filled with flowers. A huge photo of Luke kissing her was on her desk in a frame. A small envelope was next to it. She crossed the room to open it. It read:

Dearest Lily,

I enjoyed our picnic. Hope you enjoy the flowers and the photographs.

Love,

Luke

Thus, began the courtship of Lily Collins. Luke spent hours sending her gifts and flowers. He came to have lunch with her and took her to the mainland for dinners and theater. He began walking her home after work. Some days he let her cook, other days he did the cooking. They talked for hours finding they had many things in common.

A year after the accident, Luke got down on bended knee to ask Lily to be his wife. When she said yes, he whisked her off to a local eatery where friends and family waited to celebrate with them.

Now on the two-year anniversary of their meeting she was set to marry Luke Cavendish. Lily wondered in awe at the things the winter storms blew onto the beach. Never imagining she would find her true love to be one of those things.

About the Author

Rebecka Vigus is an award-winning author. She spends her time between reading, writing, crocheting, hiking, and swimming.

She is currently finishing several books and is coaching other authors. She has several to release in the upcoming years. She's writing more children's books and continues to write mystery/suspense/thriller books.

She's found her permanent home in the foothills of the Cumberland Mountains of Kentucky. Where she walks her property and enjoys the wildlife.

You can find her at Facebook-Rebecka Vigus the Writer Whisperer on LinkedIn as Rebecka Vigus.

Find her at Amazon.com, Barnes and Noble, and Books a Million or on her website: https://www.rebeckavigus.com

www.ingramcontent.com/pod-product-compliance
Lightning Source LLC
Chambersburg PA
CBHW030610310726
48979CB00003B/653
* 9 7 8 1 7 3 7 2 4 3 9 1 5 *